A Gentle
Kind of Strength

Kendall McKenna

A GENTLE KIND OF STRENGTH

First edition. November 11, 2024.

Copyright © 2024 Kendall McKenna.

ISBN: 979-8227803634

Written by Kendall McKenna.

Table of Contents

DEDICATION

To all working K9s, their handlers, and their families, no matter their branch, department, or specialty. These dogs are called *partner* by their handler, with all sincerity. Despite their working status, these dogs unfailingly become a beloved member of their handler's family. The dogs work in order to please their handlers — their partners — and never hesitate to be the first one through a door, or across an open space, to face danger. Losing a K9 to an IED, or an armed suspect, leaves all who knew them grief-stricken.

Anyone who says 'they're just dogs' has never had the pleasure or the privilege, of knowing one of these special canines.

• • • •

TMS:

Kevlar: E. I. du Pont de Nemours and Company

Bluetooth: Bluetooth Sig Inc.

Crown Vic: Ford Motor Company

Velcro: Velcro Industries

Maglite: Mag Instrument Inc.

Ka-Bar: KA-BAR Knives, Inc.

Hi-Tec: Hi-Tec Sports

National Police Dog Foundation: National Police Dog Foundation

Vans: A VF Company

Challenger: FCA US LLC

Kong: KONG Company

Styrofoam: The Dow Chemical Company

Dopp kit: Buxton Acquisition Co., LLC

Nothing is so strong as gentleness. And nothing is so gentle as real strength.

—Ralph W. Sockman

Chapter 1: An Appointment With The Vet Shouldn't Be So Complicated

"Come on, goofball," Ray said, attaching the short loop-leash to Harley's choke chain collar. The big German shepherd jumped down from the backseat of the crew cab pickup. He still surprised Ray with his agility, despite his huge size.

Harley walked obediently on Ray's left side, tail curled up over his back, tongue flopping happily from the side of his mouth. Ray gave the pet hospital's waiting room a quick glance before letting Harley enter.

"Hi, Ray," the receptionist, Valene, greeted him. "What are we seeing Harley for today?"

He headed for a chair in the far corner, putting some space between the small dogs and cats, and Harley. He was no danger to the small animals, but pet parents saw exuberant curiosity in such an enormous package, and reacted protectively, so Ray always just gave them space.

"Just his annual physical," replied Ray. "His shots need updating. He might need his teeth cleaned. I'm pretty sure he's still in great health, though."

After some clicking of the keyboard, Valene said, "Got it. It should just be a few minutes."

The smaller pets and their parents were called back, probably for appointments with one of the other two veterinarians in the practice. A few more patients entered, including a stocky pit bull. Ray was wary of the dog at first. Harley showed interest in what he considered a potential new friend. There was no telling what kind of owner the pit bull's mom was, but the dog was well behaved, despite his excitement.

Luisa, a vet tech, appeared from behind a nearby examining room door. "Good morning, Ray," she greeted, smiling warmly even before she opened the door. "Come on in."

Ray's last sight of the pit was of it on its back, paws in the air, grinning happily at the two young children rubbing his tummy. "It's always good to see a responsible pit bull owner," he said to Luisa.

"That's Mrs. Shelby and Rocket," Luisa replied. She'd worked at the pet hospital so long, she knew the life stories of all the regular clients, as well as she knew her own family's. "All her dogs are rescues, and she trains them up right. So, how is Harley today?"

Ray commanded Harley to step onto the stainless steel examination table. He was quick to comply, just like he was climbing onto a large animal weight scale. "He's fine. Runs me ragged, as always. We're here for his health certification and his shots." Luisa activated the table so Harley began to rise up from the floor. Ray touched him, talked to him, reassured him everything was okay, keeping Harley from jumping to the floor.

When the tabletop reached a comfortable height, Luisa gave Harley a quick exam, checking his eyes and ears, and combing through his fur for parasites. She smiled through the entire procedure; her love for her job and her patients was practically tangible. She typed some notes on a computer screen, then turned her ubiquitous, authentic smile on Ray. "Doctor D will be in in just a minute."

"Doctor D?" A small knot of anxiety began to form deep in Ray's stomach. Only specific vets, rigorously vetted and approved by the department, could certify Harley's health. It would be inconvenient to have to come back on another day. That was assuming another vet with this practice could meet the National Police Dog Foundation's qualifications. Harley was disciplined enough he behaved himself for any veterinarian, but he actually *liked* Dr. Federov — a little.

Hell. *Ray* liked Dr. Federov. Obviously, that fact couldn't have any influence on what he had to do now. It had taken Ray the whole damn week to get control of his anticipation, and now his disappointment was like an adrenaline crash. It hurt, he realized, physically hurt. How stupid was that?

"Doctor Federov," Luisa said reassuringly, her smile was knowing, but it didn't fade by a single watt. "His last name was a problem for some pet parents to say, so we started calling him Doctor Damien. After the first few patients' parents called him Doctor D, it stuck with the staff, too."

"Oh," Ray said lamely. Critical parts of his brain had gone numb, while others showered the inside of his skull with sparks.

Luisa disappeared back into the mysterious depths of the animal hospital. The last thing Ray needed was for the staff to realize he had a *thing* for Harley's doctor. What made it worse was the blasé use of a nickname for Damien Federov, DVM.

He lowered Harley back to the floor, sitting down on the wooden bench to wait nervously. And a little excited. Harley settled onto his stomach, giving a loud groan. Ray battled to regain his equilibrium. He needed to prepare himself — again — for his encounter with Doctor Federov, without transmitting his agitation down the leash. Damien was a damn good vet; Harley sort of liked him and shouldn't lash out just because his handler was nursing a crush.

A soft knock on the door was Ray's only warning before Damien—Doctor Federov—peered in. He found Ray's gaze and held it. Damien's blue eyes and wide smile were warm and friendly. Ray always primed himself for these first few moments in Damien's presence, but the vet's smile still made his world tilt. He automatically returned Damien's smile. Ray's heart raced, spreading a pleasant warmth all through his system. He was clumsy as he got to his feet, his weak knees making it hard to stand.

Damien greeted Harley next, entering the room slowly and quietly. Ray had always admired how Damien was able to keep Harley from seeing him as aggressive or threatening. Damien's hands looked strong and capable, everything about him was self-assured and graceful.

"How's our hero, Harley, today?" Federov asked. He called all the K9s heroes and was sincere about it.

"He just needs his annual certification, and some vaccinations updated," Ray replied in a rush, hoping he didn't sound breathless and eager.

The doctor read the computer screen, his gorgeous blue eyes moving rapidly behind his dark-rimmed glasses. Ray's gut tightened, and he swallowed hard. There was a time he would have considered the thick rims, and small, square lenses of Damien's glasses to be dorky. On Damien, they were sexy as hell.

"His rabies is still good," Federov said quietly, as Ray lifted Harley back onto the table. "He just needs all the other nasties. We can't have such a social boy getting kennel cough and parvo, can we?"

Harley sat on the examining table, rigid with tension. As a healthy dog, his vet visits were infrequent, and always involved the dreaded rectal thermometer and needle sticks. Harley knew exactly what to expect from Doctor Federov, so his defensiveness simmered just below the surface.

"How are things with you, Sergeant Lerner?" Damien asked casually, leaning a hip against the counter. He gently stroked Harley's chest with an open palm but his gaze rested steadily on Ray.

The interest in him personally startled Ray. "Same as always," he replied, searching for a way to keep the topic focused solely on Harley. One of the things he admired about Damien was the way he kept Harley so calm, minimizing the threatening feel of the office. The bitch of it was, Ray was forced to carry on a conversation with someone who made his dick wake up and express interest. "Vista goes to hell every weekend, and I get a lot of overtime taking Harley to an endless stream of drug searches. How 'bout you? Did you start work at the animal shelter on Pendleton?" Ray immediately regretted his question. He was interested in the answer, but it unnerved him to have Damien's direct attention, to be under such intense scrutiny.

"I did," replied Damien with keen pleasure. He scratched Harley with both hands now. Despite his personal delight, Damien's manner and his voice kept the energy in the room calm and relaxed. "I love it. A few of the Marines do volunteer work there. You were right, their manners and personalities are a lot like cops. I also got home for a visit."

"How did that go?" The fact Ray was genuinely interested meant he was so screwed.

Damien's smile was always wide and bright. It transformed his handsome face, turning his expression warm and approachable. "It's easy to forget how damn hot it gets there! It's warm here, too, but Vegas is a whole other level."

Two years ago, Damien had been invited to buy out the partnership of the veterinarian who was retiring from the hospital's practice.

"Do you miss home?" Ray hoped for a particular answer, even though it shouldn't matter to him.

"I miss being close to my family, but then again, communication is so seamless these days," Damien replied. Harley relaxed enough to drop down onto his belly. "I have friends here, though. And owning at least a percentage of my own practice was always my endgame. It helps that I stepped right into an existing, beneficial relationship with all the local law enforcement and military."

The retired vet had spent thirty years as one of the few who oversaw the health of the working K9s in San Diego County. The practice had searched far and wide for a doctor with Damien's particular skill sets, locating him close-by, in Las Vegas.

"I love to visit Vegas," said Ray. Harley was relaxed enough to lay over on his side now. He looked up at Damien, encouraging more scritches on his chin and belly. "But it's always good to come home. I saw the world in the Marine Corps, but there was never any question that I'd come home to San Diego." He placed his own hand on Harley's side, petting gently in a burst of affection.

"I don't blame you." Damien fell quiet. With one hand he played with Harley's mouth and ears. It had taken Ray a couple of visits to realize that Damien had already started the exam, disguising it with the show of affection. He was getting a look at Harley's mouth, teeth, and ears—each of which gave valuable insight into a dog's health—and Harley was none the wiser.

At the feel of Damien's finger brushing lightly against one of his own, Ray's heart slammed against his ribs once, almost painfully, then lost rhythm. It took all of Ray's self-discipline not to jerk his hand back and give away the powerful attraction he'd been hiding. He looked down at Damien's hand resting alongside his own in Harley's fur. The world around Ray fell away, leaving him excruciatingly aware of their closeness, imagining he still felt Damien's touch.

Thankfully, Damien looked oblivious to Ray's internal struggle as he took a good look inside Harley's ears, under his eyelids, and at his gums. "He needs his teeth cleaned," he said softly. "Make an appointment to bring him back next week and we'll get that taken care of." He went quiet for several moments.

Damien's finger brushed against Ray's again, just the lightest of touches. He couldn't look away from where their fingers curled into the black fur of Harley's saddle. Damien's hands were graceful; his long, narrow fingers were elegant. Not perfect, though, Ray mused. Damien sported several scars on his hands. Ray looked a little closer, seeing subtle scars, pale and smooth, on Damien's arms. He wanted to know the stories behind each of the marks.

"Looks like you've been tagged a few times," Ray said. It was a dangerous fucking thing to do, but he surrendered to his craving. Ray lifted his other hand, running the tips of his fingers over a shiny scar on the tanned skin of Damien's forearm.

"Yeah." Damien chuckled warmly. He stilled under Ray's touch but didn't move away. "I sacrifice some protection by wearing short sleeves. But I hate it when fabric bunches around my elbows." He wrinkled his nose for a fleeting moment, his expression emphasizing his distaste.

Ray knew he was being ridiculous, but something in his chest quivered pleasantly, sending a rush of warmth flooding through him. He was charmed by Damien's expressive features. His reaction to Ray's touch meant he wasn't uncomfortable with the touch of another man.

Shutting down that line of thought before it got out of control, Ray reminded himself the odds were that Damien was just open-minded and *tolerant*. There was very little chance he was gay.

His pleasure faded as disappointment lanced through Ray's chest, snapping him out of his stupor. With a new awareness he gave Damien's white lab coat a closer look. Ray was helpless to ignore the bulge of Damien's bicep. Most veterinarians wore long-sleeved white coats. Damien's had short sleeves, his name tastefully embroidered over the left breast in dark blue thread. It was a shade of blue that perfectly matched the color of his scrubs.

Realizing with a start he was still touching Damien's warm skin, Ray was mortified. Abruptly, he pulled back his hand. "I guess scars come with the territory, huh?" He gave a self-conscious chuckle, keeping the focus on Damien's scars, so Ray could evade his gaze.

"I've thought about covering up a few with tattoos, like you've done." Damien inclined his head toward one of Ray's forearms.

"Ink isn't for everyone." Ray extended both arms, displaying them for Damien's inspection. He ricocheted between savoring Damien's attention, and alarm at being figured out. "It *does* go hand-in-hand with being a Marine, though." He chuckled at the echo of his own earlier words, "And to a lesser degree, a cop." Ray didn't like to explain his largest, most obvious scar, or the tattoo that covered it.

Damien smirked, trapping Ray's gaze and heating his blood. "I didn't say I don't have *any* tattoos," he said playfully. "I just don't have one over a *visible* scar. Yet."

Ray didn't know how to reply, or if he even should. It felt like they were flirting with each other, but he knew that couldn't be right. Ray was flirting, despite his better judgment, but Damien was just being friendly.

None of that stopped Ray from envisioning Damien's body as the AO of an extremely thorough recon mission. It was mission-critical for Ray to locate Damien's hidden tattoos. He'd have to inspect them quite closely, for accurate future identification.

Damien's sure, capable hands smoothly inserted the ear tips of his stethoscope, pressing the chest piece against Harley's ribcage. "Heart and lung sounds are great." Damien slung his stethoscope around his neck, letting it hang by its rubber tubing. Ray's fingertips tingled at the vivid memory of Damien's warm, silky skin. He'd enjoyed touching Damien, however briefly, and wanted to do it again. Hell, he'd flirted with Harley's doctor. Both were very bad, bad ideas, so it was definitely time to get this appointment over with, and for Ray to get the hell out of there, before he made a fool of himself.

"So, what shift do you work these days?" Damien's persistent personal interest was so unexpected, Ray felt wrong-footed. Maybe this was all an overture of friendship. Ray quickly dismissed that idea; Damien was just being polite.

"Swing shift." Ray kept his answer light and friendly. It was time to pull back from the engagement and execute a polite egress. "Fifteen hundred to twenty-three hundred. I'm the senior patrol sergeant in Vista, so I get Saturday and Sunday off." Why in the hell had Ray volunteered info when he was supposed to be disengaging?

"So, when do you guys hold training?" Damien leaned casually against the work counter, directly meeting Ray's eyes.

"Once a week." It was embarrassing, how eagerly he seized anything that might extend his time with Damien. He'd come here today, determined to be professional and keep his distance, but that obviously went to hell as soon as Damien had entered the room. "We rotate through different times, so guys with different schedules can make at least three sessions per month." He hesitated for just a moment. "You should come check it out. See some of your patients in action. We train way back in the hills of Miramar." With clients who were active duty military working dogs, Damien knew the shorthand name for the Marine Corps Air Station in the city of Miramar.

"Are you and Harley competing in the regional trials a couple weeks from now?" Damien wasn't persistent. He was fucking tenacious.

Ray shifted his weight uncomfortably. The competition was a big deal for police and military K9s in California, Arizona, and Nevada, so it was heavily promoted. It made sense that Damien would have heard about it through a couple of handlers. "Yeah, we'll be there."

"Defending your title?" Damien's teasing grin made Ray's stomach quiver.

Damien's thick, glossy black hair would feel so fucking nice, sliding through Ray's fingers and against his palms. Exhaling a resigned sigh, Ray said, "Might as well paint targets on our backs, since everyone seems to be gunnin' for us this year." Harley had taken the Top Dog title in last year's trials. Ray grinned ruefully.

"I certainly can't miss that, then, can I?" Damien gestured toward a surprisingly still-relaxed Harley. "Let's get him muzzled, so we can finish up and you can get out of here."

As he took the canvas muzzle from Damien's outstretched hand, Ray almost asked him if he was interested in…what? Getting a drink, sometime? Inwardly, Ray rolled his eyes in disgust. Once the soft muzzle was on, Harley knew exactly what was up. At least it forced Ray to focus on holding him secure while Damien completed the invasive parts of the examination. The muzzle was just a precaution, anyway. Harley had never bitten anyone, outside of sanctioned training, or an on-duty apprehension. Damien finished things up by administering the vaccinations, and Ray really couldn't blame Harley for feeling a little snippy during this part.

When Harley was back on his feet and free of the muzzle, he gave himself a vigorous shake. It involved every part of his body, from nose to tail, and clearly communicated his disgruntlement, louder than a shout. Ray reattached the loop-leash, prepared to flee the room as fast as humanly possible. "So, I guess we'll see you two weeks from this Saturday?" He shouldn't back Damien into a corner, but Ray had a torrid love affair with danger. A life spent in the Marines, and as a cop, was proof of that.

"I wouldn't miss it," Damien replied, blessing Ray with one of his blood-heating smiles. "I'm looking forward to seeing you again."

Ray didn't even *start* to relax until he was back in his truck, engine running. "What an idiot," he muttered to himself. Damien's parting words meant he was looking forward to seeing Ray and *Harley*, as a team. Ray gave himself a mental ass kicking for getting all worked up, like a hormonal teenager. It was a nice fantasy, but that's all it was. Even if Dr. Damien Federov was gay—which the odds did *not* favor—he was just plain out of Ray's league.

Just as Ray was about to put the truck in gear, the ringing of his cell phone spilled from the stereo speakers, filling the cab. He glanced at his dash to determine if he wanted to answer. As soon as he saw the name, Ray thumbed the button to answer.

"Nate, my friend," he greeted. Behind him, Harley whined. "What's up?" Nathan Santiago was the swing shift patrol sergeant in San Marcos, sister city to Ray's own beat of Vista. He was only two years older than Ray, but he had ten years of seniority. Nate remained one of Ray's mentors, despite the close friendship they'd developed.

"*Buenos dias*, Harley." Nate's deep voice boomed from the speakers. At the sound of his name, Harley quieted. "Hey, man, this is Tina's weekend with the kids. Are we doin' somethin'?" Nathan and his wife had divorced amicably five years ago. They passed their teenaged kids back and forth in a pretty standard arrangement. Tina was remarried, but Nate seemed to enjoy being a single father.

"Of course." Ray would need the distraction after his disastrous encounter with Dr. Federov. "What were you thinking?" Their friendship worked because they were both social, shared several interests, but neither of them were excessive drinkers. There were a couple of dive bars they'd visit a few times a month, but the meat markets of the dance clubs were a no-go.

"Come over tomorrow afternoon, and we'll grill some steaks, have a few beers," suggested Nathan.

"Sounds perfect," Ray eagerly replied. "I'll text you when I'm leaving, you can give me a list of what you need me to bring."

"It's a plan," Nathan said, almost before Ray was finished talking. "*Adios*, Harley."

· · · ·

NATHAN'S HOUSE WAS small, but it had a great backyard. On one side of the house, the yard was a long, skinny patch of concrete, too small to be of much use for anything other than a dog kennel. When his second canine had retired last year, Nate had opted not to take on a new—young—dog. The department had given Ryder over into Nathan's care and keeping, for the duration of his retirement, putting that skinny side yard to good use.

The gate of the kennel stood open, as it did almost anytime Nathan was home. Ryder was a nine-year-old Dutch shepherd, imported from the same Danish breeder as Harley. The breeder also produced a line of Labrador retriever, in high demand for narcotics and explosives detection.

Ray relaxed in a comfortably padded deck chair, watching Ryder walk the perimeter of the backyard. Moving much slower than he had just a few years ago, Ryder favored his right hip. He still made sure all the smells in his yard were where they belonged, refreshing a few marks that no longer satisfied him.

"It might take him longer to complete his circuit," Ray said to Nathan, who stood over the deluxe barbeque grill, "but he still looks good doing it. His coat's still glossy as a crow's wing." The dark brown fur, shot through with lighter, golden brindle colors, captured the sunlight, revealing reds and golds.

Nathan studied Ryder for several moments. "Yeah, he's pretty good-looking. It shows how healthy he still is, too." Nate was a handsome man, especially now that he was forty years old, but Ray had never been attracted to him. Nathan was average height, with a compact build that disguised significant strength. His dark hair was mostly gray now, and his features only hinted at his father's Mexican heritage.

Nathan was right; when the dogs' coats lost their luster, it was really just a matter of time. And nine was old, for a working dog. It was a blessing that so many of them actually lived to retire comfortably.

"Any idea which event you'll be judging at the trials?" Ray changed the subject before he started remembering Iraq, and that one, desperate chopper ride. He rubbed absently at the large camouflaged scar on his forearm.

"They want me working the narcotics search, so I can watch for handlers overdirecting." Nathan's dog handling expertise was renowned. When the K9 Program's coordinator retired in a couple of years, Nate was considered his de facto successor. Nathan closed the lid of the grill and dropped down into the chair across the table from Ray. "It's Tina's weekend with the kids, but she agreed that making them volunteer at the trials would be good for them, so they'll be there, too."

Nathan's daughter and two sons were in their teens now. They were all good kids, for the most part, but they were still moody, self-centered teenagers. Tina and Nate were always battling to get them to put down the video game controller, or to come out from between their earbuds.

"It'll be good to see them again," said Ray.

Nathan smiled fondly. "Maddy can't wait to see Harley again," he said. "She really likes him."

"Harley really likes Maddy, too." Ray snorted. "Of course he does, she's a girl. The damn flirt," he growled.

Nathan chuckled. They were silent for a few moments, sipping their beers as they watched Ryder make his way slowly around the fence line.

It was Nate who broke the silence. "How did it go at the vet's yesterday? You didn't sound particularly excited when you answered the phone."

Ray examined the neck of his bottle. He'd known he couldn't avoid it forever. "I gotta take Harley back next week to get his teeth cleaned. He got his shots updated. He's in peak health."

"Not what I meant, Raymond," Nathan's voice hardened, "and you know it."

Ray had still been getting to know Iago, his first Sheriff's canine partner, when it started to seem like Nathan suspected the truth about Ray's sexual orientation. They'd skirted the subject for months, each dropping hints to the other, but neither having the balls to be direct. Finally, on a warm, sunny afternoon—just like this one—it had only taken a couple of beers for Ray to feel safe enough to confess his orientation to Nathan.

Tremendous relief wasn't the reaction Ray had expected, and he was taken aback. Nathan had been eager for Ray to know his orientation didn't affect their friendship. He'd been so damn scared that Ray was in denial and saying anything directly—even in support—would cause an angry end of their friendship. So instead, Nathan had dropped hints and hoped for the best. Ray had been hugely relieved, himself. He was so fucking happy he was able to be himself with this man he respected, as well as liked.

"Doesn't change the answer," Ray replied through a heavy sigh. "I got through the appointment without humiliating myself or losing an excellent veterinarian. I stayed focused on Harley, and not how the doctor's smile makes my dick hard. Mission successful."

Nathan snorted derisively, lifting his beer to his lips. Neither of them said anything as Nate stood up to check the progress of the steaks on the grill. "Your recon mission was a failure, as was your mission to win hearts and minds."

Ray barked a laugh. Nathan hadn't served in the military, but he'd picked up a lot of Ray's jargon. It gave them a sort of shorthand with each other. "That was *your* idea for my mission. Neither of those were *my* stated intent."

Nathan dropped back down into his chair across from Ray. "Not confirming Federov's orientation gives you an excuse. You don't have to make yourself vulnerable, and you don't risk rejection."

Ray cared about Nathan's opinion. He hated that Nate thought he'd been a chicken shit, and Ray needed him to understand. "We both know there's a small chance that Damien's gay. Even if he is, the odds of him finding me attractive are miniscule. Just because two guys are gay, doesn't mean they're automatically attracted to each other." He made that last bit sound snide.

"*Damien* pings your gay-dar," Nathan said, his tone almost accusing. Ray regretted his spontaneous confession after he'd just met the vet for the first time. "You're almost certain he's gay, which is why you tied yourself up in knots about it."

"I haven't—" Ray started to protest.

"You stress out for days before your dog's damn vet appointments!" Nathan interrupted, sounding incredulous. "You avoid talking about Dr. Federov, and when I force you to, most of what you say is a load of shit. You're tied in knots."

Ray growled. He scrubbed both hands down his face, running his palms over his shorn hair. "Why do you love torturing me so fucking much?" he demanded.

"I like giving you shit, the same way you like giving me shit," Nathan declared. "But this is different, Ray," he said quietly. "I've never seen you like you were the night you met Damien. And your personal life came to a standstill eighteen months ago."

Ray didn't have to ask. He'd met Damien at the K9 unit's annual banquet, a year and a half ago. His once active social life had been reduced to several aborted attempts at dating. Ray couldn't move past Damien because he couldn't stop thinking about what it might be like. "How do you know anything about my private life?"

"I never knew details about what you were up to — except for those few times you introduced me to someone — but I knew when you were dating someone, and when you were back on the market." Nathan got up and pulled two fresh beers from the ice chest. Setting one in front of Ray he said, "Obviously, I've never seen you in action, man. But, you used to start something up just often enough, I know you've got some game."

"Are you calling me a man-whore?" Ray asked with a weak laugh.

"Shit," Nate scoffed. "Cops can be some of the biggest sluts of all, and you never even got close." He paused, looking like he was searching his memory. "Matthew told me something, one time—they've got a term for it, these days. Serial monogamist!" Nathan grinned, pleased he'd retained a precious kernel of intel his teenaged son had deigned to share.

Ray could live with that. If he was honest, it was true. "Thank you?" He chuckled. "But what's all this crap got to do with why you enjoy busting my balls about Federov?"

"My point is," Nathan said with exasperation, "you're a charming fucker, who knows how to talk to people. I knew from the way you found your command presence on day two of field training that you're self-confident."

"Gee, Nate, I didn't know you cared." Ray couldn't hold back his laughter.

"Fuck you, asshole," Nathan snapped, his smile belying his words. As his expression smoothed, Nate's tone became imploring. "The night of the banquet, I was a hundred percent positive you were gonna get laid by the doc, Ray. So, whiskey-tango-foxtrot?"

What the fuck, was right. Ray sat back, staring into the distance where Ryder was sprawled out beneath an avocado tree. He took a long draught of his beer, his mind racing. Nathan wasn't going to let him off the hook without spilling his guts, but there were some things Ray couldn't say out loud. He ran a hand over the bristles of his hair again.

"I couldn't get a single word out," Ray finally blurted. His throat ached and tightened, making his voice sound strangled. "All night. He was there all night, talking to anyone who wanted to. He told jokes, and he laughed at jokes. I even had more than a little liquid courage. I couldn't say a single word to him." His mouth was dry, so Ray took another drink of beer.

Nathan sat quietly, running his fingertips over his lower lip as he studied Ray. "Huh," he finally said. "Ray, I sat across the table from you all night. There was more communication going on between the two of you than you're admitting, man. The two of you were eye-fucking each other so much, I was afraid someone else was gonna figure you out."

Ray *wished* they'd been eye-fucking, he knew how to handle that, he knew what to do with that. That night, Damien sat across the table and three seats left of him. Ray had been unable to stop staring at him, and Damien knew it. *Every time* Ray admired Damien's sharp features, smooth, dusky skin, and sexy smile, he got caught. Staring at Damien's full, reddened lips, Ray would feel his gaze like a touch. Each time he looked up, he'd be trapped by Damien's brilliant blue eyes, and knowing gaze. Ray didn't know what to do.

"He kept catching me watching him," Ray finally said, his tone morose. "I never caught him looking at me. I couldn't stop looking at him, and he knew that, but he didn't act on it. It obviously wasn't mutual." Saying those words twisted Ray's stomach until he thought he was going to puke. Mortifying was too weak of a word.

"Ha! Bullshit!" Nathan declared. He shook a finger at Ray, like he had when he'd been Ray's patrol training officer. "I saw him giving you looks that were — I don't know — hungry! What room were you in Ray?"

Ray chuckled at the exasperation in Nate's voice. It was like he was back in training, getting his ass chewed for missing something obvious. He shrugged. "I was in the room where Damien had a conversation with everyone in it. Except me." Ray's flirting had been rejected many times; he knew how to handle that.

Damien had rejected *him*. His open adoration and willing devotion had received no acknowledgment. Realizing Damien was straight, Ray had gathered the torn shreds of his pride and dignity around himself.

"You already said you couldn't talk to him." Nathan shook that critical finger at Ray again. "So why is that risk all Damien's? What if he's still waiting for you to say something to him?"

Ray thought about Damien's interest in him personally. He recalled the touch of their fingers, which Damien had initiated. During the banquet, he'd watched Damien focus his attention on one jaded deputy after another, until he'd practically owned the room.

"There's been another banquet, and I've taken Harley in for a handful of vet appointments," Ray replied carefully. He had a white-knuckled grip on his self-control, keeping his voice low, and free of emotion. "Damien is very friendly, but he never asks questions about anything more personal than my work and training schedules. He doesn't leave an opening to discuss anything besides Harley's health." Maybe it wasn't the exact truth, but it saved Ray from humiliation.

He knew from Nathan's expression that he wasn't entirely buying Ray's story. Ray's entire body was coiled tight with tension. The muscles in his shoulders, his back, and his belly ached, he'd been tense for so long.

"There's more to this than you're telling me, Ray," Nathan finally said. "I think you're reading it all wrong, but whatever." He waved a hand dismissively. Ray fought to stop himself from sighing explosively in relief. "For the moment, let's say I buy that Damien's not gay, so he's not confused as hell why — after eighteen months — you still haven't jumped his bones." They both laughed as the tension broke. Ray's cock pulsed as an image flashed briefly through his mind. Damien's lean, dark body pressed against Ray's. "What is it about Doctor Damien Federov that has you trapped?"

"What do you mean?" Ray asked, but he was pretty sure he understood. He just didn't have an answer, so he stalled.

"Everybody has at least one crush in their lifetime, where their feelings aren't returned." Nathan shrugged, holding both hands out, palms up and fingers splayed. "Unless they're an imbalanced stalker, the crush fades, their feelings change, and they move on. And it doesn't take a year and a half."

Ray rubbed his palms together. He ran one hand over his hair again. Nathan sat quietly as Ray took a long drink of his beer. "I don't fuckin' know, Nate." That was the truth.

"Hmm," was all Nathan said. They were both silent as he stood up, returning to the grill. Nate pulled off the steaks and the baked potatoes, filling two plates with food. Ryder's nose proved as good as it ever was, as he awoke from his nap and made a beeline for the table. Nathan resumed his seat, and they both began to eat, Ryder watching them intently.

"Damn good steak, man," Ray said between bites. "Like always."

"Thank you," Nathan replied. He lifted his bottle of beer and Ray clinked it with the neck of his own. "So, you and Harley ready for the trials?"

"Hell yeah," Ray answered. He welcomed the change in topic. "Harley's a working dog, all the skills they test are a part of our daily life. But you know that." He knew if he told Nate that Damien had said he'd show up, it would raise questions he didn't have answers for, so he stayed quiet.

"You also make a point of getting to training sessions, a few times a month," said Nathan. "So, you can be sure *your* technique hasn't gotten sloppy."

Ray nodded his agreement. "A few of us are also going to get together on our own time, to see if someone can spot something small we can't see ourselves, that might need some work."

"If you think it'd help, I'm willing to spend some time with you and Harley." Nathan's offer was a generous one, and Ray was grateful. "I can watch you work the obstacles, and I can catch him a few times. If he's releasing his bite, or hesitating to re-bite, I'll feel it sooner than I'll see it."

"Man, you know I'm always open to advice or suggestions from you," Ray said eagerly, grateful that he had access to such a reserve of expertise and knowledge.

"Let's meet at Oceanside Kennels several mornings this week, and next." Nathan pulled out his phone and briefly searched for a contact. "I'll call Javier and arrange to use one of the exercise fields when we're there. We can play the schedule by ear, and touch base each night at the end of shift."

"Perfect." Vaguely, Ray realized Nathan wanted to work around his schedule with his kids. "Let me know what I can do to pay you back for helping us out."

He felt Nathan studying him for several moments. Ray assumed he was coming up with ideas, so he kept eating while he waited to hear what home improvement project he'd be working on.

"You know, Ray," Nathan said, drawing out the words and pausing briefly. "Over the years, I've learned just as much from you as you have from me. Maybe more."

Ray looked up in surprise. "What do you mean?"

"The first couple of years you worked patrol, I might have been a resource for you." Nathan fed Ryder a chunk of meat and gristle. He pushed his empty plate away and leaned back in his chair. "And I probably helped you get used to being a police K9 handler, instead of a military working dog handler."

"There was a little more to it than that," Ray said, pushing his own empty plate away.

"Not as much as you think." Nathan polished off his beer. "My point is, you weren't a green kid when you came off your rotation in the jail. That Marine Corps training and combat experience showed in your performance. But the Marines also taught you teamwork, and they taught you leadership. I've learned things from you that made me a safer cop and a better supervisor."

"You picked up more than just the jargon along the way, huh?" Ray asked with a smile.

Nathan chuckled. "I like the jargon the most, though. And some of the dog training techniques you brought from the military have made our program even better. I listen to how you mentor the younger handlers, and I've borrowed a trick or two."

Ray laughed, shaking his head in disbelief. "That's funny, since I always ask myself how *you* would handle a situation."

Nathan laughed as well. "My point is, there's no quid pro quo. You've got my back on the beat, and with the K9s."

"Thanks, man. I appreciate that." Ray wondered how many people ever found out respect was mutual with someone they admired. "Are we supposed to hug it out now or something?"

"Fuck off!" Nathan gave him the middle finger as they both burst into laughter.

Chapter 2: It's Hard To Concentrate When You Know He's Watching Part 1

It was midmorning and the sun had just burned off the light cloud cover. The day would end up a warm one, but not unbearable. A long line of black and white patrol cars were parked in the shade of an oak tree grove. Clustered at one end of the line was a large group of plain looking cars, all with government license plates. The dogs and handlers could rest and regroup in safety and comfort.

Ray had both driver's side doors open on his patrol car as he and Harley rested in between stages. They were off to a good start today and he was as proud of Harley as he always was. As he rehydrated, the sweat at Ray's hairline dried, and he started to feel cooler. Harley made a noisy, sloppy mess as he lapped water from his stainless steel water bucket. When he was done drinking, Ray would take him out for a break, maybe play some tug-of-war.

"Sergeant Lerner."

Ray glanced up at a familiar voice he couldn't immediately place. His heart kicked hard inside his chest when he saw a casually dressed Damien Federov heading his direction. He wore a sporty set of sunglasses that hid his expression, but his smile was wide and friendly. The vet walked with a lanky grace, a slight roll to his hips that had Ray thinking very dirty thoughts.

"Hey, Doc," he called, forcing a polite smile onto his face as he extended his hand to shake. Ray had to play it cool. In this public venue, someone might figure out Ray had a crush, and then tell Damien. "Glad you made it."

Ray barely managed to keep his smile in place when the first touch of Damien's hand sent a powerful shock rocketing through his system. When Damien's smile didn't waver, Ray knew the feeling was on his side only. He hadn't shaken Damien's hand since the night they'd first met, and Ray had forgotten what had happened. Damien's grip was strong. His skin was soft, to Ray's surprise, but he still had several calluses that proved he worked for a living.

Releasing Damien's hand, Ray wrapped his own around his water bottle. Damien held a hand out toward Harley, allowing himself to be sniffed, but kept his attention focused on Ray. It was the perfect way to reintroduce himself, without seeming dominant or aggressive.

Harley recognized Damien almost immediately, circling him and sniffing, his tail lifted and wagging. "Harley looked great out there," Damien said excitedly, as he let himself be examined. "I'm not good at judging performance, but he seems to have done well." He wore a tight fitting white T-shirt with a distressed gothic pattern. It stretched tight across the thick muscles of his biceps and chest, clinging to the taut muscles of his narrow waist. Damien's jeans were the faded blue denim color of a frequently worn favorite pair. They hung low on his hips, fitting snug across his rounded ass, and along his firm thighs. His blindingly bright white go-fasters looked right out of the box.

Christ, Damien looked fucking amazing. He probably didn't even try, either. Ray felt grungy in his khaki and olive uniform. Self-consciously, he straightened the Kevlar vest beneath his uniform blouse and tugged at the short sleeves that strained around his biceps.

"I'm really happy with our performance," Ray confessed. "You never know what the judges see, or what they're even looking for, but *I* think Harley was perfect." He added water to Harley's bucket, hanging it from the backseat caging, ordering him into the air-conditioned patrol car.

"I *did* notice that not every dog obeyed the silent hand signals." As Damien talked, he mimicked the gestures that meant *down* and *stay*.

"Hey! Doctor Federov," Nathan called to them, surprising Ray with his sudden, unexpected appearance. "Good to see you." He shook Damien's hand vigorously. Dread began to claw at Ray stomach at the sight of Nate's mischievous grin.

"Sergeant Santiago, I'm excited to see my patients doing what they do best," Damien replied. He bestowed one of his megawatt smiles on Nathan. "How is Ryder doing these days? Is he enjoying a leisurely retirement?"

Watching Damien focus his immense charisma on Nathan, remembering Ryder's name and his status, confirmed Ray's disappointing realization. Everyone Damien spoke to became the center of his intense attention. By recalling details, he made them feel singularly special. Nathan shot Ray a significant look, obviously feeling the power of Damien's personality.

Nathan shook his head, his expression filled with affection for Ryder. "Call me Nathan, please. I have the most well-patrolled backyard, anywhere." The look he sent in Ray's direction told him to join their talk. "He might lay around in the sun all day, but the moment I reach for his leash, he's at the door and ready for a walk."

"That's good," Damien replied with seriousness. "That's a great sign that he's still in excellent health, despite his age."

"Having to take Ryder on walks is also delaying my own slide into pudgy middle age." Ray snorted at the joke, as Nathan smiled in his direction, patting his still-flat stomach.

Damien folded his arms over his chest. "Since Ryder's retired, are you here giving Ray moral support?" he asked. Ray couldn't help but admire the way Damien's shirt stretched across the breadth of his broad shoulders, displaying his fit muscles flatteringly.

"I'm judging the narcotics search," Nathan replied, glancing at his watch. "Speaking of which, I'm due over on that field to set up the vehicle we're using." He looked up at Ray, one eyebrow lifted, an almost imperceptible smirk on his face. "Harley is rock-solid today. Just like I told you he'd be." After their final training together last Thursday, Nathan had declared that Ray and Harley were practically invincible. They would have to literally give away the competition with a major fuck up.

"We've still got that damn obstacle course to deal with," Ray said darkly. Overconfidence caused complacency, which led to mistakes. "Harley is such a beast, if the judges expect the dogs to all be light on their paws, we could be screwed."

Nathan stood directly in front of him, pressing his finger to Ray's chest for emphasis. "He may not be dainty, but he's powerful, and he's fast." Nathan gave Ray's shoulder a final, encouraging slap. "He'll do great because he's eager to please *you*."

Ray nodded, silently telling Nate he got the message. "Thanks again for all your help, man."

Nathan gave them both a final wave, calling good-bye as he headed back to work.

Ray turned back to Damien, finding him with an amused smirk teasing his full mouth. Ray enjoyed laughter, but he suspected Damien's humor was at his expense. "*Nathan* respects and admires you," he said, arms still folded. "He must like you a great deal, to volunteer time helping you to prepare."

Ray remembered Nate's words about their respect being mutual, and it made him smile a little. "Nathan's a good friend. He started out as my patrol and canine handler training officer, and eventually he became my best friend. Like just now, he reminded me I make a bigger deal out of Harley's size than anyone else does."

"Why do you see his size as a drawback?" Damien asked, watching Ray through narrowed eyes, his expression thoughtful. "He's got enviable coordination, and he stands out from the crowd."

Ray shrugged, considering Damien's question. "Well, this competition is open to military working dogs, and it's hard not to be self-conscious with all the delicate little Belgian Malinois prancing around."

Damien didn't immediately reply. Unfolding his arms, he tilted his head to the side, his brow furrowing just slightly. To Ray, he resembled a bewildered puppy. It was pretty damn cute. "You're joking about the delicate, prancing Malinois, aren't you?" Damien asked dubiously.

"Oh, hell yes," Ray answered emphatically. "I was a dog handler in the Marines, too. My partner was the *best* damn Belgian Malinois bred anywhere." He rubbed at the lingering phantom pain beneath the large scar on his arm.

Damien laughed. The sound sent a fission down the length of Ray's spine. "You can't let Harley, the magnificent German shepherd know that, of course. He'd see it as a betrayal."

A loud whine came from inside the patrol car. It was like Harley actually understood their conversation. Chuckling, Ray glanced at his watch as he said, "We're second up for the Agility round, so I'm gonna give His Lordship a quick break." As he opened the rear door to secure Harley's leash, a voice boomed over the arena's PA system.

"As his doctor, I'm happy you're keeping Harley hydrated. It's a pretty warm day, and his activity level is unusually strenuous." Damien took a few steps back, giving Harley space to exit the vehicle.

It seemed like Damien was reluctant to end their conversation. Ray's imagination was getting overactive again. At least he hadn't made a fool of himself, this time. "Okay, we're on deck," Ray said distractedly. "But we can talk more in between events." He enjoyed Damien's company; he had from the beginning. Ray even felt like he was getting used to having Damien's attention focused on him.

"I look forward to it," Damien said, already walking backward in the direction of the grandstand seats. "Is it okay to wish you luck?"

"Since we're not on patrol duty, that's perfectly appropriate." Ray couldn't help what he knew was his goofy grin. Beside him, Harley was on all fours, ears forward, tail lifted. He was already back on duty, waiting for Ray to issue a command; any command.

"Good luck then." Damien paused. His expression was smooth, but he tilted his head to the side inquiringly. "Just out of curiosity, what would I say if you *were* heading out to start your shift?"

"Be safe." Ray knew he wouldn't have to explain further.

"Roger that." Damien gave a brief wave of one hand, turning to head back to his seat.

Ray tossed his empty water bottle into a nearby blue bin. As much as he didn't want to, he had to lock down any and all thoughts of Damien Federov. It was time for Ray to shift his focus. He pulled up his mental checklist of the equipment he needed for the obstacle course. Harley would start out on leash, but Ray would release him early on, and clip the short leash to his belt. He wore a spare leash like a baldric, out of the way but easy to deploy if needed. Harley's "baby" was stuffed in a leg pocket of Ray's olive-green uniform pants.

Ray watched Harley run around the grassy clearing that was set aside for giving the dogs breaks. He was proud of the big goofball today. Harley was energetic and focused; all their hours of training had definitely formed a strong foundation. A single thought of Damien slipped through, and Ray realized his use of military jargon must mean the Marines at the animal shelter were rubbing off. Smiling to himself, Ray called Harley to heel.

When they reached the arena gate, a female petty officer out of North Island still had about a third of the course left to complete. Ray led Harley out about ten feet, giving the petty officer plenty of room to exit without the dogs becoming distracted by their own curiosity over each other.

He turned to face the arena gate. Harley immediately assumed the down position, before Ray needed to give the command. That was a good sign. Ray just had to hold up his end of things, and not give Harley conflicting signals.

Sensing motion from the corner of his eye, Ray resisted the urge to look over and scan the spectators. Now was not the time to be thinking of Damien, let alone trying to spot him. Ray wondered how the hell he was supposed to concentrate now, with Damien watching from the grandstand.

The petty officer completed the obstacle course, praising her partner in an excited, childlike voice. The crowd erupted, cheering enthusiastically, as the handler vigorously scratched her dog's neck and back. The announcer's voice boomed from the large speakers that surrounded the arena. Ray ignored the words that filled the air around him, waiting to hear his own name cueing him to enter the arena.

The gate monitor leapt into action, providing the petty officer with an egress. Once she and her partner were clear, Ray stepped forward. Harley was immediately on his feet, his body a tight coil of potential energy just waiting to explode with excitement. Together, Ray and Harley stepped into arena, as the disembodied voice introduced them.

"This next team is the defending champions from last year. In addition to winning several individual events, they took the overall title of Top Dog! From the San Diego Sheriff's Department, please welcome Sergeant Ray Lerner, and his canine partner, Harley."

The crowd cheered, several ear-splitting whistles carrying over the cacophony. It was like the roar of the crowd was magically converted into raw, physical energy. The air around him seemed to move, pushing Harley and him forward onto the field of battle. A rush surged through Ray, setting fire to his competitive nature.

"If there's a dog handling gene in our DNA, Sergeant Lerner was born with it. During his eight years in the Marines, he was a military working dog handler, serving in both Iraq, and Afghanistan. Lerner has been with the Sheriff's Department for eleven years."

As they reached the starting line, Ray sensed the gate closing behind them. The first proctor was a San Diego PD officer who looked familiar to Ray. San Diego was hosting the trials, so most of the staff and volunteers were from local law enforcement agencies. Ray knew them either through the local network of handlers, or he'd worked directly with them.

"His canine partner is a four-and-a-half-year old German shepherd named Harley. Sergeant Lerner is Harley's first handler, but Harley is Sergeant Lerner's second Sheriff's canine partner. This team has worked together since Harley arrived in America from Denmark, when he was only eighteen months old."

The proctor verified Ray and Harley were ready to start. He glanced around the arena, making sure the three judges were paying attention, and that everyone was in their places. Everyone in the arena signaled that their section of the course was clear. Harley was down on Ray's left side, intense and eager, staring upward as he waited for a command. Ray unhooked Harley's short leash, clipping it to a loop on his own tactical belt.

"Harley is cross-trained in protection, tracking, and drug detection. And because he's from Denmark, and also received his basic protection training there, you'll hear Sergeant Lerner giving Harley his commands in Danish. Once again, this is San Diego Sheriff Sergeant Ray Lerner and Harley."

"Whenever you're ready," the proctor said, backing away from them.

Harley's nose was still pointed upward, as he focused all of his attention on Ray. He displayed no curiosity about the course, or any concern about the other people in the arena with them. His entire being was focused directly on Ray, just like he needed to be.

Without a word, Ray stepped onto the course, breaking the timer's laser beam and starting the clock. Like most of the events, this one was timed. The goal was to make it through the obstacle course, completing each task correctly, in the least amount of time. The three judges would add penalty seconds to the final time for each mistake they observed. Ray's goal was to get through this stage quick and clean.

Ray didn't have to command Harley to heel. As soon as he moved forward, Harley was on all four paws, excitedly walking beside him. Their first obstacle was a set of four three-foot-high jumps, three of which were made to resemble walls or fences. The fourth was a large square, cut from the center of a tall piece of plywood. Ray sent Harley with a single command and a hand gesture and came to a stop.

Harley sprinted ahead. He sprang upward, effortlessly, gliding over the first jump. Landing lightly, he maintained his stride until he reached the next jump. Harley sailed easily over each wall and didn't hesitate to launch himself through the simulated window. Ray stood tall, mentally crossing his fingers that Harley was falling back on all those hours of training.

The moment his paws returned to earth, Harley spun around and ran in Ray's direction. Passing him on the right, Harley pivoted behind Ray, coming to sit down on his left. It was a perfect execution of the obstacle.

Ray reached down and rubbed vigorously at Harley's chest, leading him to the next obstacle. He lavished praise on his dog in a high-pitched voice, using baby talk and childlike endearments. Harley pranced excitedly beside him, basking in the praise and eager to do whatever Ray wanted him to.

Ahead was a ladder leading to a platform, six feet from the ground. Ray sent Harley up the ladder. The platform was eight feet long, but only two feet across. Harley was steady and graceful as he walked along the platform. At the midpoint, Ray halted him with a verbal command. Harley froze in his tracks. Ray waited only long enough to demonstrate that Harley wouldn't complete the obstacle until commanded to. He called Harley down the ramp at the far end of platform. He was silently pleased that Harley showed no hesitation, and no fear. Leaping down from the ramp, Harley rejoined Ray at the heel.

They moved forward as Ray rubbed at Harley, telling him over and over he was such a good boy. They reached the next obstacle and Ray stopped. Harley dropped into a sit, watching Ray with obvious anticipation. This obstacle had worried Ray, since Harley had begun to show signs that he was going to be a large, heavy dog. Taking a deep breath, Ray tried to relax, and let his confidence in Harley bleed through. If he communicated doubts to Harley, Ray would be the one who fucked this up. Harley *could* do this, Ray had seen him pull it off dozens and dozens of times.

Four boards of graduated heights stood in a row. The shortest board was six inches tall; the last one was twelve inches. The entire arrangement was six feet long. Ray was always worried that Harley would have trouble getting his extra heavy neck and chest over that distance.

He gave Harley the command. Without hesitation, Harley ran toward the obstacle. He was a fast dog, and he reached his full speed in just a few strides. Harley pushed off with his hind legs, fully extending his entire body. He was graceful and fleet, quickly sailing over the jump in one smooth motion.

Landing gracefully on the far side of the obstacle, Harley immediately turned toward Ray. He circled once, coming to sit on Ray's left side. As far as Ray was concerned, Harley's execution was perfect. He told his dog how perfect he was, that he was such a good boy, and that his daddy loved him.

The next obstacle was the A-frame, and it was just what it sounded like. Two ramps connected at the top by a small platform. Harley had never struggled with this, nor did he this time. He landed lightly on the ground and immediately rejoined Ray, sitting at the heel.

One last obstacle and they were done. The plywood box was eight feet long, four feet wide, and sixteen inches high. Ray gave Harley the command to crawl through the box, and he entered the obstacle without hesitation. When he emerged out the other side, Harley immediately returned to Ray's left side.

No matter what their final time was, no matter how the judges scored them, Ray considered Harley's performance flawless. He couldn't be more proud, and he told Harley with his voice and his hands.

They broke the beam of the laser, stopping the clock. Ray couldn't hear their time over the cheering of the spectators. Harley was a fun dog to watch while he worked, and people seemed to like him. He didn't really care about their time, anyway.

Ray and Harley exited the arena as a handler with San Diego Police waited to go in. Several people called congratulations, or good job to them. Ray thanked them graciously, as he hooked Harley's leash to his collar.

Reaching the patrol car, Ray poured a fresh bottle of water into Harley's bucket, opening one for himself. Now that he could afford to let his concentration lapse, and his mind wander, Ray wondered about Damien. He knew where Ray's patrol car was; was there a chance he thought Ray was interesting enough to come talk to him again? Ray thought he had a better idea now of where he might stand with Damien. He felt more comfortable talking with him. And since his crush was just as strong as it ever was, Ray *wanted* Damien to search him out.

As these thoughts swirled chaotically through his mind, Ray watched Harley splashing everywhere as he lapped up his water. It took his stomach rumbling for Ray to realize he was hungry. Looking at his watch, he calculated the time, hoping he'd have time for lunch before he was up in his next stage.

"You two aren't competing, you were showing off."

Ray smiled at the sound of Damien's now-familiar voice. His heart raced, warmth spreading through him. He looked up to watch Damien approach them, a wide smile on his face. "Harley just does things exactly how he was trained to do them," Ray replied. "But I admit, I'm very proud of him."

"I'm impressed with both of you." Damien leaned over, scratching at Harley's neck and chest. "You're firm and confident when you give Harley his commands, but you're steady and calm. You don't give ambiguous or conflicting commands, so he understands what to do. You come across calm and confident, so he trusts you and doesn't hesitate."

Ray suddenly knew just how Harley felt when he received Ray's approval and praise. Damien had his sunglasses on top of his head again. He openly studied Ray with brilliant blue eyes, his full lips parted in a smile that revealed his perfect, straight, white teeth. Ray waited for Damien to lose interest and move on, but in the meantime, he enjoyed being this close to him. "That's down to training," he said. "Hours and hours of training. We work hard to master good techniques that don't unconsciously confuse our dogs. The rest just comes with experience."

Ray was able to admire the smoothness of Damien's dusky skin. He wanted to touch, to see if it was as silky—everywhere—as it looked. He thought he could smell Damien's cologne, but he wasn't sure they were close enough to each other.

"As Harley's doctor, I have a clearer idea of the types of injuries he might sustain. I also understand what unique issues he might face as he ages." Damien idly scratched Harley's chin. His hands were masculine looking, the veins on the backs making them even sexier. Harley was in bliss as he enjoyed the chin scratching. He rested his head against Damien's thigh, his eyes half closed. "And I also understand the type of body mass he needs to have. We really need to make sure he keeps off excess weight."

Ray was gratified and relieved at Damien's observations. He knew Harley's future health was in good hands, and if Ray had concerns about anything, Damien would understand.

Before Ray could reply, he caught the mouth-watering scent of meat grilling on a barbeque. "Christ, that smells good," he said, completely distracted. He glanced in the direction of the forming line. "I need to find out when Harley's scheduled for his next two events, so I know what time to have lunch." Ray expected Damien had already arranged to have lunch with someone interesting. Still, his mother and the Marine Corps had insisted he have manners. "Are you hungry?" There was nothing suspicious about Damien and Ray hanging out, and getting lunch together, either. Harley was one of Damien's many patients.

"I'm hungry, but I can wait a little while for the two of you." Damien's answer made him seem prescient. He couldn't be eager to have lunch with Ray, could he? Maybe Damien was interested in having a friendship.

"Let's go check my schedule then." Ray opened the rear door of the patrol car. "Harley, hup," he said. Harley immediately jumped into his compartment inside the vehicle, curling up for a restful break.

Chapter 3: It's Hard To Concentrate When You Know He's Watching Part 2

Ray checked the schedules. He had enough time for lunch before their next event. He even had the time he needed to give Harley more water and a final break.

"Does this happen at all the competitions?" Damien asked, as they stepped into line.

"Yeah," Ray answered. "It's a successful fundraiser for the K9 Program. The department's budget for us covers dog food and healthcare."

"I've always wondered about that!" Damien exclaimed. "So, the department *does* reimburse you for Harley's office visits and his vaccinations?"

Ray nodded emphatically. "We file expense reports for reimbursement. We can request an advance, if we're aware of some sort of upcoming large expense."

"Or your friendly veterinarian gives you a paid invoice, *before* he collects payment," Damien said conspiratorially, grinning slightly.

"That's a cool thing to do," Ray said with a grin. "Anyway, what we make from the barbeques allows us to purchase special training equipment, or it goes toward hosting this competition."

They took their plates full of food and found seats at one of several wooden picnic benches. The table filled up around them with handlers from various agencies. As Damien was recognized, handlers expressed their gratitude that he'd come out to see the competition. One of the Marine dog handlers recognized him from the Camp Pendleton animal shelter.

With the dogs as common ground for all of them, Damien was instantly a part of their social group. He embellished some of the stories handlers told. Damien was animated as he shared medical knowledge, or a firsthand follow-up to an incident. Just like he did at the banquets, he easily held everyone's interest. The intensity of Ray's attraction to Damien was stronger, now. He'd already fallen under the spell of Damien's personal charisma, but from now on, it was going to be a hell of a lot harder to hide his feelings. Ray doubted that a friendship with Damien would make that any easier.

When they were finished with the meal, Ray still had plenty of time to get Harley ready to go and make sure he was focused on his job. It was Ray whose head wasn't in the game. He enjoyed Damien's company and wanted him to stay around.

He should probably get control of his emotions. If he couldn't control them, Ray needed to ignore them. With his brain on Damien, he was in danger of fucking up Harley's performance. Cops were trained observers, so it wouldn't be long before they'd start to notice and speculate about Ray's distraction. If anybody made a connection between Ray and Damien, so what? They were both adults, and both single, and anything between them was perfectly appropriate. Except he didn't want Damien finding out about Ray's unrequited crush; that would be too fucking humiliating.

"Criminal apprehension is next for you two, right?" Damien fell into step beside him.

"Yeah, it is," Ray answered. "I have just enough time to get Harley squared away and warmed up."

"I can't wait to see Harley in action." Damien's smile was going to fucking kill Ray. Then, he caught his own lower lip between his straight, white teeth. "He seems like he enjoys chasing down and chomping on bad guys," Damien said playfully.

"He does, yeah." Ray sounded breathless to his own ears. He gave a self-conscious chuckle. "I can't say I blame him. Catching bad guys is fun."

A corner of Damien's sensuous mouth quirked upward. "Will I get to see you being tough, and handcuffing the criminal that Harley apprehends?"

Ray knew he was losing his grip, because it felt like Damien was flirting. How the hell was he going to stay focused during the event? He knew he'd be thinking of Damien when it was time to handcuff the agitator. "Yeah. At the end, Harley has to stand guard while I secure and search the suspect." Ray shifted his weight nervously.

"Sounds like fun for everybody," Damien said with a smirk. "I'm going to head back to my seat, and let you get back to work. See you afterward."

Ray called something in reply, but he couldn't be sure what it was. Christ, he had it bad. Things were hard enough when Ray had considered Damien a capable veterinarian, and a good-looking man. Now that he knew Damien was also witty, personable, smart, and a little flirtatious, he was in danger of becoming obsessed.

He got Harley out of the patrol car and began running through all of his mental checklists. If they were working a shift, neither Ray nor Harley could afford for him to be distracted by his crush on Damien. It was time to get his shit together.

Ray made sure they were both hydrated. He released Harley in the clearing, letting him run, play, and stretch. From a leg pocket in his olive colored tactical pants, Ray produced Harley's "baby." The favorite toy was a thick, brightly colored rope, tied into a couple of knots. Harley spotted his toy and excitedly tried to get it from Ray's hand.

They played a short game of tug-of-war. Ray threw the rope for Harley to fetch. The exercise seemed to get both of them back into the right frame of mind. Harley's toy also served as a reward, and he was ready to do whatever Ray asked, so he could have his toy.

He heard his name called over the PA system, letting him know it was time to head toward the arena. The next announcement had Ray and Harley on deck. They watched a team from the San Diego Police Department go through the event stage. Harley lay beside Ray, alert and ready for action. He paid no attention to the gunfire in the arena, just like he'd been trained.

Ray wouldn't let himself look into the spectator stands. He told himself his occasional glances were accidental. Trying to locate Damien in the crowd was a bad idea. It was a needless distraction, and it was too difficult, anyway. Ray glanced into the stands again, unintentionally, locating Damien immediately. Glancing away quickly, Ray took a deep breath and focused his attention on the arena again.

The SDPD team finished the event and headed for the gate. When they were clear, Ray started forward, Harley right beside him. They were a team who typically excelled at this event, and Ray refused to be the one to fuck it all up.

The event proctor, a retired sheriff's deputy, greeted Ray, explaining the first stage of the event. Downrange, one of the newest young handlers on his department was dressed in a full bite suit. He moved with the familiar waddle of someone swathed entirely by marshmallows.

Ray downed Harley, giving the command to stay. Then he held his breath. Harley stared down range, his ears completely forward. He was poised to launch himself, if Ray gave him the command.

The agitator turned around, clumsily, and started to run. Harley visibly twitched, starting to get to his feet. Remembering himself, he dropped back down onto his stomach, crawling forward only a few inches. Down range, the agitator stopped running, turning back to face them. Harley whined but stayed in the down position. Ray was as proud as always. With Harley's "baby" in hand, he lavished praise on his dog for a job well done. They played tug-of-war briefly, until Harley got the rope away, and chewed on it vigorously. The reward of the toy kept Harley from getting frustrated at not being allowed to chase down a suspect.

The arena was reset for the next obstacle. Removing the leash, Ray hooked his fingers in Harley's collar. This was a clear signal, and Harley responded. He lunged against Ray's grip, barking aggressively. In the real world, this display was meant to intimidate suspects into complying, instead of running or fighting.

"Sheriff's Department with a canine," Ray shouted. "Do not run. If you run I'll release the dog, and he will bite!" Harley knew what the announcement meant, and it fired him up even more. He really liked his job.

The agitator turned away and ran—as well as he could wearing a marshmallow body suit. Ray released Harley's collar, and the dog was off like a shot. When he'd closed about half the distance to the agitator, Ray shouted the command for Harley to end his pursuit and return to the heel. Mentally crossing his fingers, Ray counted on the endless hours of Harley's training. None of the dogs liked to be called off before they'd made the apprehension, but it was crucial for the handlers to have this kind of control. Harley didn't let Ray down, either. He dropped out of his all-out run, loping in a wide circle until he was lying on his belly beside Ray.

Throwing down the rope toy in front of Harley, Ray praised him vigorously for his perfect performance. Harley chewed on his rope, his tail wagging, as he basked in Ray's approval. He was reluctant to give up his toy, so there was a brief game of tug-of-war before Ray finally got it back.

He took hold of Harley's collar again. Down range, the agitator shouted aggressively at Ray. It simulated a real-life situation, at the same time it got Harley's attention. Again, he lunged against Ray's grip, barking loud and menacingly.

"Sheriff's Department with a canine! Do not run. If you run, I'll release the dog and he will bite!"

The agitator turned and ran. Ray released Harley, shouting the command to stop the suspect, as he followed at a run. Harley was nearly a blur as he closed the distance to the fleeing suspect. At the last moment, the agitator turned, braced for impact, and offered one heavily padded arm. Harley launched himself from several feet away, colliding with the suspect as he sank his teeth into the bite suit.

Bracing his forepaws against the suspect's body, Harley held tight to his arm, shaking his head back and forth viciously. The agitator resisted, pretending to fight Harley. Aggressively swinging a light stick, the agitator shouted angrily at Harley, striking him gently on the side with the stick. Harley wasn't intimidated. He held his grip on the suspect, digging his paws into the ground, refusing to give ground. Ray stepped within a few feet of the struggling pair, ready to pull Harley off the agitator if he had to. He shouted the command for Harley to release the bite and heel. Harley growled, giving another vigorous shake of his head. Ray was just about to reach in and pull him off when Harley released the bite on his own. He trotted around to lie down next to Ray, a wide smile on his face, and his tongue hanging from the side of his mouth.

Leaving Harley in the down position, Ray ordered him to stay. Stepping up to the agitator, he pretended to conduct a body search of the *suspect* and take him into custody. Harley watched the process with a singular intensity. He was poised to intervene if the agitator fought or ran. He stayed in the down position, though, like he was supposed to.

Ray praised Harley for his perfect performance, letting him play with his rope. All the long hours of training showed, making them worth it, all over again. They were nearly done, and Ray had complete faith in Harley.

The arena was reset, but before Ray could make his announcement, the agitator fired two blank shots from a small handgun, and then turned to flee. Harley took off in pursuit of the suspect. He hadn't flinched, and he hadn't hesitated; he'd charged directly toward the danger.

The agitator fed Harley a sleeve, bracing himself against the strong thrashing. Ray commanded Harley to release the bite. He put Harley in the down position, stepping in to secure the suspect. This time, the agitator pretended to attack Ray. The moment the *suspect* made a move toward Ray, Harley was on his feet, launching himself at the agitator. Again, he growled aggressively, shaking his head violently. Ray waited several seconds, letting Harley enjoy himself, before calling him off. On command, Harley released his bite, returning to lie down beside Ray.

It was a perfect performance. Ray's praise was drowned out by the cheering crowd. Attaching Harley's leash and letting him have his toy rope, Ray turned to leave the arena. He resisted the urge to look toward the crowd, to spot Damien. This event was over, but he still had work to do, taking care of Harley. He'd managed to put Damien out of his mind before; he'd do it again.

After a drink of water, and quick break in the clearing, they moved on to their final event of the day. During their timed searches, Harley was quick to locate the suspect—hidden in a large, wooden box—and the drugs hidden in a car. He made no false alerts and hit on the targets on his first passes. Ray dragged Harley around by the rope toy as he chewed on it happily. Whatever their place in the standings, he was perfectly happy, and he couldn't be more proud of Harley.

Just as Ray was tucking Harley into his compartment in the patrol car, Damien reappeared. Ray couldn't help his wide grin.

"You two are pretty impressive," Damien called, smiling openly.

"Thank you," replied Ray. "It was all Harley, though. I just held his leash." His face warmed, and he hoped he could blame it on the sun.

"From what I've learned today, you just hold his leash now, because you've already put a lot of hours into his training." Damien inclined his head toward the patrol car. "Is the champion getting his rest?" he asked, grinning.

Ray relaxed back against the vehicle. "Yeah. He's earned it today." His stomach tightened pleasantly, as he watched Damien watching him. The trials were over, so Ray allowed himself to enjoy Damien's company. Harley wouldn't need to make a visit to the veterinarian for several months, so after today, Ray had plenty of time to get over his crush.

"He lives to make you happy," Damien said on a sigh. To Ray's surprise, he came to stand beside Ray, also leaning back against the patrol car. "It's obvious, even if you're not looking for it, that he follows your commands precisely, just to earn your praise."

Ray's heart swelled with pride. He and Harley had worked hard together. It had all paid off, and he was so damn happy. "Today was important for getting the dogs certified, but how they behave on the job is even more important. I trust Harley when we're on patrol. I know I can count on him."

"It's nice to have a big trophy that shows that to the world too, though." The corner of Damien's mouth lifted playfully again.

Ray's attention was trapped by Damien's full mouth. He shook himself out of his stupor, hoping Damien didn't notice his distraction. "That's far from a sure thing." Ray finally tore his gaze away from Damien's handsome face.

"That's not false modesty talking, either," Damien mused. Ray wasn't sure what he meant. "I think you're going to be surprised. You're popular among the spectators, too."

Ray barked a surprised laugh. "Were you taking a survey?"

"I didn't have to," Damien replied with a laugh. "Several ladies were very vocal in their admiration. You probably wouldn't have any trouble getting them to express it to you directly."

Ray's heart leapt into his throat. He stared off into the distance, trying to keep his expression smooth, shrugging dismissively. Ray swallowed against a tight throat, hoping Damien would find something else to tease him about.

"The young deputies who were watching from the stands have probably all moved in on that territory by now," Damien surprised Ray by saying. The teasing ended without any awkwardness between them, to Ray's relief. "Genuine humility isn't a very common trait, you know. People find it attractive. The young deputies were talking amongst themselves, about how helpful you are to them. I guess not every veteran cop takes the time or effort to share their experience and knowledge. They respect and admire you."

Ray was always willing to mentor new deputies, and dog handlers. He just never knew it was significant to anyone he'd helped. "That's good to know," he said, looking over at Damien. "It's gratifying to know your efforts are appreciated."

The PA exploded to life, announcing the scores were tallied and the standings and awards would be announced in five minutes. It was time to retrieve Harley and head for the arena.

"I'll just say congratulations now, in case I don't get the chance afterward." Damien extended his hand for Ray to shake.

Confusion warred with disappointment as Ray reluctantly clasped Damien's hand with his own. "Congratulations for what?" He frowned in confusion.

With a shrug, Damien replied, "Whichever awards you've won today. You and Harley both deserve them."

Perplexed, he watched Damien slowly stroll away. "There's no guarantee we won anything."

Damien's only answer was a brief wave and a quick smile over his shoulder. Ray stood feeling alone. Harley's deep sigh from inside the patrol car dragged Ray back into reality. Retrieving his dog from his compartment, Ray headed for the arena.

He was extremely proud of Harley for winning both the narcotics search, and the criminal apprehension stages. Tucking the two medals into his pockets, Ray started to plan his egress from the venue, ready to get Harley home, fed, and tucked up in his kennel for the night.

A fellow deputy won third place overall. Ray clapped and whistled for his fellow handler, pleased that young deputy and canine had performed so well. He was still offering his congratulations when the winner was announced.

"And finally, taking the title of Top Dog...with the San Diego Sheriff's Department, Sergeant Ray Lerner, and K9 Harley!"

Astonishment kept him rooted in place when Ray heard his name called along with Harley. He received several slaps to his back and shoulders before someone finally gave him a firm nudge toward the judges.

The trophy was five feet tall, topped with a golden figure of a German shepherd. It resembled the trophy they'd won the year before but was slightly different. Harley had no clue what was going on, but he eagerly lapped up all the praise and attention. Maybe he'd have to stop for a hamburger on the way home, so Harley could have a special treat.

By the time all the photographs had been taken, Ray had shaken a dozen hands, and expressed his gratitude to everyone he could think of, and the sun was setting. He'd kept an eye out for Damien but had never caught sight of him. Ray was acutely disappointed. Maybe he'd call the office on Monday, ask Damien how he knew, and thank him for...for what? Just hanging out in between stages? He had a couple of days to figure that part out.

His plan for a quiet evening at home quickly changed. Nathan suggested all the handlers go out for a celebratory dinner. After everyone took their dogs home, of course. The group was fun and social, so Ray was happy to join them.

He glanced around at his surroundings once more. Ray thought that if he could find Damien, he'd invite him along to dinner. It made sense to include one of the vets, as a valuable member of their team.

Nathan carried the trophy to the patrol car, while Ray kept Harley on the leash. "I invited Damien," Nathan said as he put the trophy in the trunk. Ray closed Harley inside his compartment inside the vehicle. He looked up abruptly, surprised. Nathan closed the trunk and came around the side of the car. "I told him where and when we'd be tonight. He said he'd meet us there."

Ray's mouth went dry, and he struggled to swallow. "What exactly did you say to him?"

"I told him we were going out as a team, to celebrate all the recertifications, and all of the great individual performances," Nathan replied, leaning back against the side of the vehicle. "I said I wanted him to join us, since his help in keeping our dogs healthy is invaluable."

Deciding the invitation was sufficiently neutral, Ray relaxed a little. He still didn't quite trust Nate not to drop hints at Damien. "Did you know he sometimes provides paid invoices to handlers, *before* he gets paid?" It still amazed Ray that Damien, and the hospital, would think to make something like that easier on a cop.

Nathan looked surprised. "No, I didn't. That's pretty fucking awesome." Ray nodded his agreement. "Anyway, Doctor Federov certainly knows you're alive. And you no longer have any trouble talking to him. No more excuses."

Ray snorted, shaking his head in disbelief. "Yeah, it looks like we might be able to be friends." Before Nate could reply, Ray stood and reached for the handle of the driver's door. "I gotta get Harley home. I'll see you at dinner."

"You better show up. I don't think the good doctor is coming out just to spend time with his patient's handlers." Nathan said loudly, stepping away from the patrol car.

"I already said I'd be there!" Ray gave a brief wave as he pulled away and headed home. He had a couple of hours to come up with things to talk about with Damien, that didn't make him sound like a lovestruck teenager.

Chapter 4: Good Food, Good Friends, and a Little Flirting

Another burst of raucous laughter filled the restaurant. It looked like Damien was eagerly following the activity at the far end of the table, eyes and smile both open wide. Ray had no idea what was going on, but he enjoyed watching Damien having a good time.

The opening bars of "Happy Birthday" rose up around them. Ray turned to see who tonight's victim was. He laughed at Dave Riggs' disgruntled expression. A veteran deputy, a few years from retirement, with a fondness for practical jokes, Riggs got prickly whenever the tables were turned on him. Someone had managed to get to the restaurant staff first, arranging the public humiliation for Riggs.

"He sure looks pissed that someone remembered his birthday," Damien said in a low voice, leaning closer so only Ray could hear.

Ray caught a hint of Damien's musky scent, imagining he could feel the warmth of his skin across the distance. Hiding his smile behind his hand, Ray replied, "It's not really his birthday. Riggs is known for arranging public spectacles to embarrass people. We're all fair game. When anyone manages to turn the tables on him though, Riggs is a notoriously bad sport."

"That just makes it more fun to target him," said Damien, chuckling.

Ray leaned in closer, lowering his voice. "I pretended to enjoy the attention. I flirted with the waitresses, which earned me a few hugs, and I refused to share the dessert they set in front of me. I haven't been targeted since."

A slight chill spilled through Ray as his own words registered. His comment about flirting with the waitresses was too easy for Damien to misunderstand. Shit. If he tried to elaborate, he'd just sound defensive and idiotic.

"What happens when it *really* is your birthday?" Damien asked, sipping at his cup of coffee. "You're not stuck, hiding out alone, I hope." He'd become serious abruptly, his expression looked genuinely curious.

Ray wondered what it really was Damien was hoping to uncover. "I don't feel the need to make a big deal out of my birthday, but I'm gracious when family and friends go to the effort to recognize it."

"You must have some family living local, since you're originally from these parts." Damien's expression politely curious. His demeanor was suddenly more formal than either of them had been since they'd sat down beside one another.

For an instant, Ray thought he'd upset Damien, prompting him to throw up some barriers between them. Whatever intuition helped him read people correctly on the job told Ray that Damien's sudden tension was anticipatory. "My parents, two sisters, and some assorted cousins," he answered, cradling his own coffee cup between both hands.

"Do they have photos of you and your dogs hung all over the house?" Damien asked without a hint of mocking. "Does your mom keep a scrapbook of the news articles that mention you?"

"You've met my mom?" Ray asked around his laughter.

Damien's laughter rolled warmly through Ray's system, twisting his stomach into knots of pleasure. "Does she make sure your dates know how lucky they are to have your attention?"

Ray's chest tightened as his stomach lurched. His pulse started to sprint when his brain told his body that something good might be going on here. Was Damien looking for confirmation because Ray tripped his gay-dar? Maybe Damien just wanted to know if Ray had his family's support.

"I haven't introduced very many men to my parents." Ray was careful to keep his voice low. He paused to sip his coffee, working hard to appear relaxed and casual. "The few that have met my family not only had to endure my mother's scrutiny, but both of my sisters, too."

Damien showed no reaction at first. He continued to meet Ray's gaze directly. "It's usually the other way around, isn't it?" he asked, smiling warmly. "Is either sister married?" For the briefest moment, Damien dropped his eyes to Ray's mouth.

"Both are married with kids. And neither husband got off easy, either." Ray chuckled into his coffee, remembering what he'd put both of his brothers-in-law through. He wanted to look over at Damien now, to see if he was satisfied with the answers Ray had given him.

Their conversation was interrupted by the waitress' return to the table. She began handing out leather folios containing their meal checks. Damien thanked her when she set the dark faux leather folder in front of him. Ray watched the waitress glance inside the next folio to verify the check inside, before reaching to place it in front of him.

"Grab that, Doc, before Lerner gets ahold of it," someone called out from the far end of the table. Ray wondered what was going on, as he reached for the folder with his check. Before he could get his fingers on the thing, Damien's hand appeared and snatched it away. It was several moments before Ray's brain caught up, connecting the things he saw and heard.

"Got it," Damien declared, giving Ray a smirk. He held the folio in the hand away from Ray.

"I appreciate the thought, guys," said Ray, holding his hand toward Damien in a silent request for his check. "But it's not necessary."

The folio was taken from Damien and passed around the table, hand-over-hand. "It's not necessary, but that won't stop us," Nathan said when Ray's check landed in his hand. Good-natured laughter rose up from around the entire table.

He glanced at Damien to find him openly grinning at Ray. His face flushed warmly when Damien's gaze lingered on him. "Thank you, gents," Ray said, glancing around at his fellow deputies. Several called their congratulations again, and Ray thanked them graciously.

As the guys got their bills paid, they said their good-byes and headed home. As the group dwindled, Damien finally stood up, pushing in his chair. Ray followed him, like it was a compulsion. Nathan shook their hands, and then turned to herd a few younger deputies out the door. Quiet settled over Damien and Ray as they were the last two members of their group left inside the restaurant.

"What are your plans for the rest of the evening?" Damien asked as they slowly made their way toward the exit together.

"I was just going to head home," Ray answered. He hoped Damien's question held intent, rather than idle curiosity. "What are you thinking of?"

"I don't live very far from here," Damien replied quickly. "You could come have a beer, or I could make coffee."

Harley had been fed and was tucked up in his kennel for the night. Ray didn't have to be home anytime soon. He reminded himself that he was getting way ahead of himself, thinking Damien was offering anything more than a coffee between two friends.

"Coffee sounds good, since I'll have to drive home," Ray said, holding the door open for Damien to exit. Stepping out into the clear, cool night air was pleasantly refreshing. He and Damien crossed the parking lot side-by-side. It felt companionable. They spoke in hushed tones, as if an enchantment had settled over them. Damien moved closer, brushing their shoulders together unselfconsciously.

"Go ahead and follow me to my place," Damien said quietly after he'd disarmed his car alarm. He reached out and clasped Ray's hand, giving a brief squeeze. He smiled warmly, making Ray's stomach tighten pleasantly.

Ray's mind was racing as he climbed into his own car. He struggled to believe that Damien wanted more than friendship with him. Following Damien home meant Ray wanted the same thing. He had no idea when and how things had changed between them. He had no idea how he'd missed it happening.

• • • •

DAMIEN'S HOUSE WAS small, but attractive and homey. It seemed right for an unmarried professional who worked a lot of hours. That's probably why Ray saw more than a few similarities between his own home and Damien's.

While Damien started the coffee, Ray found himself drawn to numerous photos displayed on a number of hanging shelves. Despite the dim setting Damien had set the lights at, Ray could easily see happy people enjoying the fun activities. He made out several people with dark hair and blue eyes that had to be Damien's family.

Appearing beside him, Damien handed Ray a mug of coffee. It was pale colored, just like he liked it. Taking a small sip, he was pleased to find Damien had taken him seriously. Ray took a lot of shit from other deputies for preferring his coffee with a lot of milk and sugar, but he didn't give a shit. He liked it how he liked it, and Damien had mixed the coffee perfectly.

"That's really good. Thank you," Ray said, taking a longer pull on the mug.

"Glad you like it," said Damien, smiling. When he lifted his own mug to his lips, Ray saw it was also very pale in color. "I like a little coffee with my milk and sugar."

Ray chuckled quietly. He was amazed to realize he and Damien shared a lot of common ground. Their similarities made things comfortable between them, and Ray surprised himself at how easily he relaxed in Damien's company.

"These have to be of your family." Ray gestured toward the photos with his coffee mug.

"It *is* kind of obvious, isn't it?" Damien's fond smile made his affection apparent. "Our genetics are pretty powerful."

"How many siblings do you have?" Ray was sure he could identify ten individuals of Damien's generation.

"I've got an older brother and two younger sisters," he surprised Ray by replying. "My parents each have a brother they're very close to. We grew up with six cousins who are all the same ages and who look just like us."

"You guys are lucky." Ray and his sisters got along with their cousins, but none of them were particularly close.

"Two of my cousins are gay, so it made coming out a lot easier." Damien pointed to two men in a large group photo. "We had each other for support and we were a united front when we actually came out to the family."

"How'd that go?" Ray had come out quietly to his sisters, so they'd had his back when he'd dropped the bomb on his parents.

"A lot of the family took it in stride, some were surprised and just needed a little time to adjust to the idea." Damien lifted a shoulder in a negligent shrug. "A few older members of the family are still hostile. Part of their anger has to do with the realization that they don't have the power or influence over the family they thought they had."

Ray nodded his understanding. He had a couple of in-laws who hadn't been happy to discover the family's response to ultimatums wasn't in their favor.

One of the candid photos captured Ray's curiosity. Damien eagerly shared the story behind the moment of hilarity, frozen in time. Ray was acutely aware of how close Damien was as he talked. The warmth of his body seeped into Ray's arm where Damien brushed his chest against him. Lowering his voice to just above a whisper, Damien murmured the end of his story against Ray's neck. His breath was warm and smelled of coffee, raising gooseflesh on Ray's body.

He turned his face toward Damien, admiring his full and shapely mouth. Ray wanted to taste Damien's lips, and to feel his warmth along the full length of his body. He watched in silent fascination when Damien leaned in. At the feel of Damien's lips against the side of his throat, Ray gasped, his heart leaping in his chest.

His fingers were numb and he gave no resistance when Damien relieved him of his empty coffee mug. Ray watched Damien dispose of both mugs and then return to where he stood. It might be a hell of a surprise, realizing his attraction to Damien was reciprocated, but there was no doubting or denying it any longer.

When Damien stepped in close, Ray reached for him. He cupped the base of Damien's head, tugging him forward. Wrapping his other arm around Damien, Ray grasped his firm, rounded ass. He pressed himself against Damien's body, rocking his hips rhythmically. Lowering his head, Ray met Damien's mouth with his own.

There was no surprise, no hesitation on Damien's part. He rocked against Ray's body, feeling willing and eager. Snaking his arms around to hold their chests tightly together, Damien parted his lips, meeting Ray's tongue with his own. A feast for the senses, Damien was warm and velvety, his masculine musk flavored with coffee and cream. At the very first taste, blood flowed into Ray's prick.

Ray changed his angle, deepening the kiss. Damien breathed heavily, his warm breath dancing over the skin of Ray's cheek. A soft moan vibrated in Damien's chest, spilling into Ray's where they were pressed together. Licking deep into Damien's mouth, Ray teased his tongue, lapping at the roof of his mouth.

Breaking the kiss, Ray nipped at Damien's throat. He licked at the pulse, hammering violently beneath Damien's flushed skin. "Show me to your bedroom," he whispered hoarsely against the shell of Damien's ear.

Taking a step backward, Damien tilted his head to bare his vulnerable throat for Ray. His hands were firm and strong on Ray's back, encouraging him to move forward. The dim light cast their surroundings in shadow. Stumbling through the house, they collided with a few corners and walls. Ray refused to be deterred from diving back into Damien's mouth.

He was vaguely aware when they stumbled into the small bedroom dominated by a wide bed. Soft light from the hallway spilled through the door, illuminating the things Ray needed to see. He put a little space between their bodies, reaching for the buttons of Damien's shirt. He was distracted by Damien's searing kiss, and the grip of his hands on Ray's ass.

Finally, he got the damn shirt open. Ray admired the smooth skin of

Damien's chest, running his palms over firm muscle.

"Since you brought us here," Ray murmured, pushing Damien's shirt off of his shoulders, "I'm guessing you have the supplies we need." He nipped Damien's swollen lips, giving soothing licks in between.

"I've got the basics," Damien whispered into Ray's mouth, stepping backward toward the waiting bed.

Ray followed, even as reality tried to infringe on the perfect moment. Fleetingly, he wondered what Damien wanted from him. "So, what do we do now?" Ray managed to ask, despite Damien nipping at his earlobe. A pleasant shiver dashed through his body.

Damien's low chuckle was a damn sexy sound. His breath drifted warmly over Ray's throat. "You don't *really* need me to tell you how all this works, do you?"

Damien's tone was playful, but Ray's face still flushed hot with embarrassment. He huffed a self-conscious laugh. "I know how things work. I just don't know how things work with *you*. Or how you *don't* want them to work." Ray didn't care what Damien liked; he was up for it. He'd get his own pleasure from making Damien happy.

"Mmmm," Damien hummed, his voice breathy. "I can tell from your touch and your kiss that I'm going to enjoy anything you want to do." Slowly, he sank down onto the foot of the bed, kissing a moist path along Ray's body. Damien skillfully unfastened Ray's belt, lightly slipping his fingers beneath the hem of his T-shirt and lifting.

Complying with Damien's silent request, Ray lifted his arms for his shirt to be lifted up and off. Ray savored the warm skin of Damien's naked chest against his own, skimming his fingertips over Damien's back and shoulders.

His already swollen cock pushed harder against Ray's fly as it was flooded by another rush of blood. Watching Damien, knowing his intent, made Ray's knees weaken with desire. His rapid breathing sounded harsh in the quiet room as he carded his fingers through Damien's thick hair.

"If we're both naked, I can take care of you at the same time," Ray managed to say, despite the dryness of his mouth and tightness of his throat. He was never selfish about his own pleasure, and he wanted Damien to know that.

Spreading open the front of Ray's jeans, Damien pressed a moist kiss to his hipbone. "I don't need this to be quid pro quo. Just do what feels good, when you feel like doing it." Damien emphasized his point with a flick of his tongue into Ray's navel.

How literally did Damien mean that? Because Ray really liked the idea of sliding himself deep into Damien's ass. His train of thought derailed when Damien reached in, pulling Ray's hard-on out of his skivvies. Clenching his jaw, Ray battled the impulse to fist Damien's hair and shove his cock past those sexy, kiss-swollen lips.

He sucked a deep breath in through his teeth as he watched his dick slide into Damien's welcoming mouth. The heat and the wetness surrounded Ray's hard-on. He slid the silky strands of Damien's hair between his fingers as he struggled. Ray struggled not to break the grip of Damien's hands on his hips even as he reveled in tight suction and the flicks of his tongue.

Admiring Damien's long lashes, sharp cheekbones, and sensual mouth, Ray traced his fingers along where his own cock stretched Damien's lips. Christ, it felt good. It would be so easy for him to spill into Damien's mouth, but Ray was determined to hold himself back. He wanted to be balls deep in Damien's ass when both of them came.

His hands itched with the desire to hold Damien still and fuck his mouth vigorously. Ray had no idea if that would be welcome, and he wasn't going to do anything that might jeopardize this fragile thing between them. He had a sensitive and a gentle side, and Ray wasn't embarrassed to let anyone see either one.

"Jesus, that feels good," Ray murmured. As he admired Damien's handsome features, Ray traced them lightly with his fingertip. "You're so gorgeous. You make me feel so good. I wanna make you feel just as good."

Ray's breath caught when Damien looked up at him, humming around his cock. His blue eyes looked feverish, the widened pupils giving him an ethereal appearance.

Heat flooded Ray's belly as his hips flexed harder, against his will. A shiver ran down his spine and his balls lifted and tightened. Ray threaded the fingers of one hand through Damien's hair, gripping his shoulder with the other. "Not yet. Not yet," he said breathlessly. "Not without you too." He hoped that made sense to Damien.

Pulling off with a gasp, Damien grinned up at Ray. "If you insist." As he began to slide up the bed, Damien managed to kick off his blue-patterned Vans.

Ray braced a knee between Damien's legs, reaching for the fly of his jeans. The bulge of his erection was obvious. He was surprised when Damien abruptly leaned up, wrapping his arms around Ray's back. They tumbled onto the bed together, limbs entwined and heavy breaths mingling. Ray covered Damien's body with his own, fusing their mouths as they licked into each other deeply.

As Ray tried to urge him farther up the bed, Damien buried his hands down the back of Ray's jeans. Damien's strong hands gripped his ass, relentlessly pulling him down, urging him closer. The rough texture of Damien's jeans rubbed against the sensitive underside of Ray's cock, sending a fission up his spine. He moaned into Damien's mouth, obeying the demanding dig of his fingers in Ray's ass.

He broke the kiss with a wet smack, trailing his lips along the underside of Damien's jaw. "Come on and slide up the bed for me," he whispered. Ray pressed up onto his hands, hovering over Damien. "I want you naked so I can feel your skin against mine. I wanna make you feel good."

Damien gasped, a shiver wracking his entire frame. "Jesus fucking Christ," he whispered. Suddenly, he was wriggling out of his jeans and kicking them to the floor. As Damien managed to slide the remaining distance to the head of the bed, Ray struggled out of his own shoes and socks.

Ray shimmied out of his jeans as he crawled up the length of Damien's body. He admired Damien's hard-on, taking it in one hand and giving it a firm stroke. "You are so fucking gorgeous," he rasped. "Tell me how to make you feel good—how to make you happy." Releasing Damien's cock, Ray covered his body with his own. He thrust his hips, rubbing himself against Damien's slick, warm skin. "Shit. I'm fucking dying to be inside you. Will you let me? Will you let me fuck you?"

Damien writhed against him. He stared up at Ray with a hungry expression, thrusting his hips upward. "I've enjoyed all our flirting, but I want more. I wanna know what you enjoy. I wanna feel you inside me." Damien surrendered with such ease; he left Ray stunned. Parting his lips, he met Ray's tongue with his own. He wrapped his arms around Ray's back, moaning softly.

Sliding his lips sensuously over Damien's moist ones, Ray swallowed down each of his debauched sounds. With his chest heaving, Damien's warm breath drifted lightly over Ray's cheek. Gliding his fingers over Damien's face, Ray buried them in his hair, fisting the silky strands.

"Say it." Ray recognized an edge of desperation in his own voice. Something inside him enjoyed the idea of corrupting Damien.

"Godammit, Ray!" Damien growled, an edge of anger coloring his tone. "I want you to fuck me!"

Ray vaguely wondered how much control Damien might be willing to surrender, when they'd built some trust between each other. For now, though, he was going to lose himself inside Damien.

Chapter 5: Some Things Are Better Said With Touch

Kneeling naked on the bed, Ray's erection stood out from his body, aching painfully with the height of his arousal. His balls hung low between his legs, so full and swollen they felt ready to burst. Damien and he were both so turned on; their bodies radiated heat, their skin slick with sweat.

As he watched Damien intently, Ray breathed harshly through his open mouth. He skimmed his palms along Damien's inner thighs, feeling his entire frame quaking in response. Damien lay supine, hands braced over his head, his legs falling open toward his sides. His chest heaved as he desperately dragged air in through his parted lips. The muscles in his thighs and his stomach quivered each time Ray touched him.

Damien's cock was long and thick. The shaft was a dusky rose color; the wider head was darkened almost purple. His engorged hard-on lay curving against his belly, its darker shade contrasting with Damien's olive skin. Watching Ray through heavy eyelids, Damien's body was tense and straining with arousal and anticipation.

Ray pressed a slick thumb to Damien's puckered opening, feeling it clench tighter as a tremor rolled through his body. Damien gasped softly, exhaling a quiet moan. Ray circled Damien's hole, spreading lubricant teasingly. Pushing gently against Damien's fissure, Ray felt him cant his hips slightly in encouragement and longing.

"Not yet," Ray murmured. He moved his hand to cradle Damien's ball sac, smiling when he heard a frustrated moan.

"I'm ready," Damien said, his voice low and hoarse. "I know I am. I've been ready."

"I'm making sure you're slick and loose," Ray replied, grinning down at Damien. Even in the dim light, Ray saw a flush on his cheekbones. "So, I can bury myself inside you with a single thrust."

Damien writhed, dropping his legs open further. He pressed his palms against the headboard again, his body trembling even more. Ray watched Damien's asshole tighten and relax, over and over as he shifted restlessly. He'd slicked Damien hole so he knew he was relaxed, but Ray wanted him turned-on and out of his mind with desire.

Retrieving the bottle of lubricant, Ray coated his fingers again before tossing it aside. Slowly, he crawled up the length of Damien's body. He placed open-mouthed kisses on Damien's stomach, and the sensitive skin over his ribs. Dragging his tongue across Damien's chest, Ray nipped lightly at his flexed muscles, and budded nipples. He glanced up at Damien's face, making sure he was watching Ray's every move.

With his free hand, Ray braced himself above Damien. He lowered his head to press his face to the warm, moist skin of Damien's throat. Ray swiped his tongue over the hammering pulse in Damien's neck and nipped sharply at his straining tendons. Pushing two lubed fingers into Damien's hole, Ray pressed inward until his palm met heated skin. He stretched Damien's opening with his knuckles, slowly fucking his ass as he spread the lube.

Turning his face to the side, Damien bared his neck for Ray, like an invitation. Ray mouthed a path up the length of vulnerable flesh. He nuzzled the tender, fragrant place behind Damien's ear before taking the sensitive lobe between his teeth. Ray worked his hand quickly. He pushed deep into Damien's body, giving his gland a light, glancing touch, for now. Sliding his fingertips to Damien's opening, Ray tugged at his rim, stretching the ringed muscles and easing Damien open.

Ray lavished Damien's ear with loving attention. Beneath him, Damien's body stiffened, a tremor rocketed through him like he'd been struck with a powerful bolt of lightning. Ray suckled Damien's earlobe, dragging his teeth along its length. Slowly, he traced the firm tip of his tongue over the sensitive shell of Damien's ear, triumphant at the feel of another shiver coursing through him when Ray exhaled a warm breath over the moistened skin. Damien rode Ray's three fingers vigorously, murmuring filthy words of encouragement. Ray met each thrust eagerly, pushing his fingers deep into Damien's ass.

Teasing Damien's sensitive ear, Ray enjoyed the way his pleasure echoed in the clench and release of his inner muscles. When he pushed back against Ray's hand, Damien's hole opened easily, his ass eagerly taking Ray's fingers deep. The constant flow of passionate whispers was broken only by Damien's harsh, audible breaths. His body quaked, over and over, beneath Ray, as Damien moved his legs restlessly. He probably wasn't aware of his own desperate words, but Ray wanted to hear more. Each flick of his tongue, every grind of his hips was meant to keep Damien drowning in pleasure, and begging Ray for more.

Ray slid his fingers free of Damien's hole, starting to reach for the bottle of slick. Damien was suddenly everywhere, his arms and legs embracing Ray, pulling him closer. The heat of his body enveloped Ray, Damien's gaze, his warm breath seemed to reach right into Ray. Giving in to the tug of Damien's arms around his torso, Ray lowered himself onto his forearms. He licked deep into Damien's mouth, breathing in each of his harsh exhalations. Ray flexed his hips, sliding his cock along Damien's erection and the warm skin of his belly. Damien wrapped his strong legs around Ray's waist, pressing his calves into Ray's ass cheeks, encouraging him to move.

Needing to catch his breath, Ray broke the kiss with a wet sound. Damien writhed beneath him, breathing heavily through his parted lips. Ray struggled to steady his breathing. He stared down at Damien's open expression, amazed to see the blue of his irises obliterated by his pupils, blown wide with arousal. Ray buried his fingers in Damien's hair, enjoying the silky feel of it against his fingers.

"I'm ready," Damien said in a harsh whisper. He skimmed his hands restlessly over Ray's back. "I'm ready for you." He pulsed his hips rhythmically, rubbing eagerly against Ray, teasing his cock with a pleasant friction.

Ray moaned, struggling for patience. He pressed an open-mouthed kissed to the moist skin of Damien's throat. "Gotta make sure you're ready," he said in a low, gravelly voice. "I want you nice and slick and relaxed." He nipped at the underside of Damien's jaw.

A shiver ran through Damien's body in response. "I'm ready," he said fiercely. "I have been. You're just a fucking tease." A hint of frustration bled into his voice.

Ray smiled against Damien's heated cheek. That's exactly how he wanted Damien—aroused, eager, and impatient. "Need to be sure you're ready for me. Don't wanna go too fast."

Damien moved fast, catching Ray off guard. He dug the fingers of one hand into Ray's ass cheek, reaching between them with his other. Ray hissed at the intensity of Damien's touch, his spine arching in pleasure as he thrust his cock into Damien's hand. Squeezing his eyes closed, Ray clenched his jaw, battling to control his body's reactions. "Oh fuck," he whispered harshly through his gritted teeth. "Fuck, fuck, fuck, fuck." Damien's grip on Ray's dick was firm as he jacked him quickly.

"Jesus! I need you inside me." Damien arched his neck, watching Ray with heavy-lidded eyes. "I need you to fuck me."

Damien's words were maddening. Ray's cock ached from the fresh rush of blood to the head, his shaft pulsing against Damien's firm grip. He was ready to be inside of Damien, so Ray released his grip on Damien's hair. He was surprised to find his fingers were stiff from his tight grip, and Damien seemed to really like it. Christ, he was as eager and desperate as he'd wanted Damien to be.

"Gotta get myself ready." Ray was done with the teasing. Reluctantly, he pushed himself away from Damien's body, resting on his knees. He retrieved the bottle of lubricant, and the condom from the tabletop where he'd placed it.

"Want some help?" Damien asked in a low voice. He skimmed his hands up and down Ray's thighs, running his calves over Ray's hips and ass. It was like he couldn't stop moving. Damien smirked playfully, his kiss-swollen lips lifting at the corners. His darkened eyes smoldered as he watched Ray's every movement.

With a breathy chuckle and a trembling hand, Ray struggled to thumb open the lid of the lube bottle. "Having your hands on my dick might end everything, before it really gets started." He used his teeth to tear open the condom wrapper.

"You've got better self-control than that." Damien snatched the bottle from Ray's shaky hand. "Better self-discipline."

From anyone else, that would have sounded to Ray like a challenge. Coming from Damien, Ray knew it was understanding that came from simple observation. "Don't underestimate yourself," he said in a growl. He looked down the length of his own body to watch Damien touching him. Ray's cock was dark red, standing out rigidly from the dark hair at the base. He watched Damien skim his graceful hand over Ray's chest, sliding his fingers through the chest hair. His breath caught in his throat, and Ray's erection gave a violent twitch. "See? Won't take you long at all."

"Lube first? Or just the condom?" Damien asked. He ran his palm down Ray's stomach.

Ray tightened his abs reflexively, his cock bounced as if demanding Damien's attention. He struggled to focus on Damien's words, instead of his desire to have Damien's hand on his dick. "Lube, yeah. On the head," Ray answered slowly, his tongue feeling thick with desire.

The coolness of the gel was a shock when it hit the head of his dick. Ray hissed, his cock bouncing as he clenched his muscles in response. Damien snatched the condom from Ray's limp fingers. Settling the latex over the slick tip of Ray's erection, Damien used both hands to slowly unroll the condom. Ray moaned loudly, enjoying the sights and sensations of Damien's fingers delicately caressing his shaft.

Needing to hold on to something—anything—Ray grasped the insides of Damien's thighs. He released a shaky breath as Damien slid the tips of his fingers up and down Ray's dick, extending and smoothing the rubber. Damien stroked gently, almost teasingly, along Ray's length. A playful smirk still danced along Damien's lips as he nudged the edges of the condom into Ray's pubic hair, at the base of his cock. A shiver ran the length of Ray's body and he reflexively tightened his grip on Damien's thighs. Giving a tortured groan, Ray clenched his jaw and silently begged his body not to come. He wasn't sure he was going to survive Damien's final addition of lube to Ray's erection.

"Are you done teasing?" Ray asked, voice strained.

Damien's expression grew serious again. "Yeah," he replied, sweeping his eyes hungrily over Ray's face.

Taking a deep breath, Ray squeezed the base of his erection, trying to keep himself under control. He found himself wrapped up in Damien's arms and legs and pulled down steadily onto his body. Ray braced one forearm on the pillow beside Damien, still holding onto his own cock with his other hand. Damien's body was on fire, his heated skin felt good where he was pressed against Ray's chest and stomach.

Ray lined up the head of his cock with Damien's slick asshole. Their harsh breathing melded, echoing loudly through the bedroom. Damien held him close, his gaze locked on Ray's. The sudden intensity of this intimacy scared the hell out of Ray, but he refused to close his eyes, or look away. He wanted to watch Damien's handsome, expressive face as Ray pushed into his body.

Bracing both forearms on the pillow beside Damien, Ray steadily pushed his hips forward. Beneath him, Damien took deep breaths, his body relaxed and pliant. Ray felt no resistance as Damien's hole opened easily, letting him slide his cock in smoothly.

His cockhead was suddenly enveloped in delicious heat, Damien's inner muscles clenching Ray tight. "Fuck!" he said in a harsh whisper, his gut tightening at the onslaught of sensations. He watched Damien closely, enjoying his changing expressions. When Ray pushed into Damien's ass, stretching his hole, Damien's eyes widened. He gasped, his mouth falling open as he breathed heavily in between moans of pleasure.

Ray rocked his hips rhythmically, working his cock deeper and deeper into Damien's ass. Finally, Ray's erection was totally enveloped in Damien's heat, the tight muscles of Damien's channel gripping him tight. "Christ, you feel good," he murmured.

He started to move, using his back and thighs to power the firm thrusts of his hips. Damien's heated breath danced over Ray's lips and cheeks as he exhaled each time their bodies met. They moved with each other, and against each other, Damien eagerly matching Ray's motions.

Damien moved restlessly, his arms and legs encouraging Ray's movements. He canted his hips so Ray easily sank his cock all the way to the hilt. His harsh exhalations became guttural, animalistic sounds of pleasure and exertion. "Oh fuck, that's good," Damien blurted. His eyes looked glazed, his mouth hung open, and he gripped Ray's ass cheeks with both hands.

Ray was captivated by Damien's response and was suddenly driven to elicit more of them from him. He slid his fingers into Damien's hair, fisting the strands. Ray loved the way Damien arched his neck in response, his eyelids falling closed, as he gave a low moan of pleasure.

"You like this?" he asked, placing a line of biting kisses along Damien's jaw. Ray tugged sharply at the hair in his grasp, feeling Damien's groan vibrate between them and flow into his own chest. "You like it when I do this? What else do you like? Tell me what you want."

Ray shifted his legs on the bed, changing his angle and getting better leverage. With a hard thrust, he buried his cock deep in Damien's ass. It was obvious he did something right when Damien cried out, his eyes snapping open wide. Ray gave a few slow, teasing thrusts, before pushing in hard and fast again. Damien's shout tightened something deep and low in Ray's gut, pushing him toward his own orgasm.

Arching his back, Damien pressed himself against Ray's chest and stomach. He ran his hands up Ray's back until he could curl them over his shoulders. "Like this," he said, in between Ray's hard thrusts. "Yeah. Just like this." Damien let his thighs fall to his sides, opening himself wider to Ray.

Their skin was slick with sweat. Each time Ray fucked into Damien's ass, their bodies slid along each other. He was surprised at how sensual it felt, having Damien's cock pressed between them as his stomach rubbed back and forth along the shaft.

Ray used his grip on Damien's hair to keep his neck arched as he pounded into him. The hardness of Damien's erection slid against Ray's lower belly, as he fucked Damien's hole. His thighs and hips ached as he angled his cock to brush against Damien's gland with each stroke. Damien's expression held pure pleasure as Ray watched him closely. His eyes were closed; his mouth hung slack as sounds of ecstasy escaped him each time Ray was buried deep in his ass.

Damien's body tightened around him; he clung harder to Ray with his arms and legs. "I'm close," he said in a raspy voice, his brows drawn together in concentration. "Jesus, I'm getting close."

Ray growled low in his throat, nipping along the edge of Damien's jaw. The desperation in Damien's voice, the intensity of his expression tugged hard at Ray. Heat and pressure built up fast, low in his belly, rolling through his hips and into his balls. The base of his spine tingled and he knew he was going to follow Damien right over the cliff. "What do you need?" Ray asked, nuzzling the damp hair at Damien's temple.

Tightening his legs around Ray's hips, Damien arched upward against him. His cock pressed more firmly to the sweat-slick skin of Ray's belly. "Keep moving," Damien said through gritted teeth. "Don't slow down."

Ray was happy to oblige. A shudder ran through him as a tingling spread from his spine, through his hips. He was flooded with warmth, and something low in his belly knotted pleasantly. His balls tightened slightly, as they swung freely with the flex of his hips. "Getting closer?" he asked in between gasping breaths.

"Fuck yeah." Damien's voice was strained. His expression was intense, like he was solely focused on chasing his pleasure. He opened his eyes and finally managed to focus on Ray's face. Damien's pale eyes were obliterated by his wide-open pupils. "How close are you?"

"Getting damn close," Ray managed to answer. His ass and thighs burned with exertion. Ray's own climax was pretty fucking close now. Gooseflesh rose up all along his skin, and his balls eased closer to his body.

"Oh fuck!" Damien gasped, his eyes going even wider. His grip on Ray's body was almost painful as he clung to him. "I'm coming!" he said on an exhale. "I'm coming!" Damien's body vibrated, his breathing even more harsh. His inner muscles clenched and released Ray's cock, as Damien's orgasm ripped through him. Pleasure suffused his expression as he cried out loudly.

Damien's cock pulsed violently between their bodies. As damp heat coated his chest and stomach, Ray caught the sharp scent of Damien's come. His breath caught in his chest as sparks scattered inside his skull. Burying himself deep inside Damien's ass, Ray's body locked up tight. His balls pressed against his own body as his cock pulsed, and a violent shiver ran down his spine.

With the first spill of fluid from the tip of his dick, Ray's muscles spasmed. He opened his mouth to shout with pleasure, but no sound came out. He watched Damien watching him, as they both rode the endless waves of their climaxes. Even as Damien began to relax, Ray's back arched involuntarily and his breath locked in his chest. He saw his own intense pleasure reflected in Damien's expression. Stars danced in the gray shadows at the edges of his vision.

Ray's body gave out on him, refusing to move with any coordination at all. He collapsed onto Damien, pressing his forehead into the pillow beside him. Their breathing was rough and harsh, as they both tried to regain control.

Awareness returned to Ray slowly. Damien didn't seem to mind Ray's weight, since he kept his arms wrapped loosely around Ray's back. Pressing a kiss beneath his ear, Ray gently slid himself the rest of the way out of Damien's body, careful to secure the condom. He stumbled sluggishly from the bed to the bathroom, disposing of the used latex. It was easy to find a clean cloth that Ray soaked with warm water.

Damien was still sprawled limply across the bed when Ray sat beside him, beginning to clean off the drying come.

With an appreciative sound, Damien opened his eyes. He smiled warmly up at Ray. "You don't have to do this. I don't expect you to clean up our mess."

"I want to," Ray said, returning Damien's smile. "I know I'm sufficiently butch that I'm okay openly showing affection." His chuckle sounded almost giddy. "Also, I didn't bother to ask if you enjoy the bottom, so I owe you some TLC."

Damien covered Ray's hand with his own, stilling his motions. His expression was bemused as he smiled lopsidedly. "I like the chivalric attitude,"

Damien said in a playful tone. "And you asked me the most important question." He released Ray's hand. "Everything after that was toe-curling fun."

Ray huffed an embarrassed laugh, secretly pleased with Damien's pronouncement. As he returned to the bathroom to dispose of the cloth, Damien's wicked chuckle trailed after him. Back in the bedroom, Ray slid into bed beside Damien, the sheets warm from his body.

With his head on the pillow next to Ray's, Damien sighed deeply. "It's a good thing I only ever wanted to be a vet, 'cause I suck at reading people," he said, his tone sounding playful. "I read you completely wrong."

Ray had no clue what Damien meant. He blamed his confusion on postcoital stupidity. Damien sounded happy and relaxed, but the dim lighting made it too damn hard for Ray to read his expression. "What did you read in me? Why do you think you got it wrong?" Considering how this night had gone, Damien had read Ray pretty damn perfect. "I'm sure you read people just fine. They tend to like you, so they want you to like them, as well. It makes things pretty straightforward." He felt like he was babbling. It was that postcoital stupidity again.

Burrowing deeper into the bed, Damien curled his arm up under his pillow. "It took me forever to get a solid read on you, though. You've been a Marine, now you're a sergeant, and a dog handler, so I was sure you'd be a 'take charge' kinda guy. I dropped hints that I was interested, expecting you'd make a move, but I read you all wrong."

Ray snorted in surprise. "When did you drop hints that you were interested? What were the hints?" he asked incredulously. "I thought you were just being nice to the handler of one of your patients." He was starting to feel like an idiot, for working so hard to hide his crush. "How long have you been hinting at me?"

Damien groaned, burying his face in his pillow. "I suck at this worse than I realized," he said mournfully. "Since the very first time you brought Harley in for an appointment."

Taken aback by Damien's revelations, Ray stared at him mutely, wishing for a little more light. He thought about all the shit he'd told himself—that Damien wasn't gay—that his friendliness was professionalism—deluding himself into believing he didn't have a chance. "I convinced myself you couldn't possibly be interested in me." Ray chuckled ruefully, running a hand over his face. Nathan was going to relish this opportunity to gloat. "Am I such a dick that it seems like I need to always have control?" Being in control turned Ray on, but so did pleasing his lover, ensuring he was well satisfied.

"No. No!" Damien replied hastily. "You've never been a dick to me. You're a pretty intense guy," his voice sounded rough and tired. "Formidable is probably a better word. I convinced myself you didn't like aggressive men, so I had to stick to flirting and just be patient. I told myself you'd read the signs and make an approach when you were ready." His lips twisted in a rueful grin.

Ray studied Damien, still reeling from the realization that his feelings were reciprocated. His gut tightened slightly when he thought about how close he'd come to fucking everything up. "Well, obviously I'm not afraid of an aggressive man." And if Ray didn't step up and finally be the strong, aggressive man Damien expected and wanted, he could still fuck it all up. Ray smiled, impulsively lifting a hand to brush a few stray hairs off of Damien's forehead. "But apparently, I'm not very bright, and my ability to read people with any accuracy ends the same time as my work shift."

Damien's eyes grew heavy lidded at the touch of Ray's fingertips. He adjusted his position, so they lay closer together. "I wager I just suck at subtle flirting." Damien lifted one corner of his mouth in a teasing grin. "We're a hell of a pair, convincing ourselves we couldn't possibly have what we really want." As he caressed Ray's chest with one hand, Damien's fingers threaded through the dark hairs.

Lifting one hand, Ray twined his fingers with Damien's, keeping their hands pressed to his chest. "We should get some sleep. We'll need our energy so we can remind each other it's okay to have something—someone—we really want."

Damien languidly rolled over but making sure to keep their hands joined. He quickly doused the bedroom light, rolling back over and into Ray's arms. "I might need some extra convincing tonight, and then again tomorrow morning."

"I'm happy to make that sacrifice," Ray said, pressing a kiss to Damien's temple, before he settled in and slept.

Chapter 6: An Infrequent Quiet Weekend At Home

It was a gorgeous summer day; the clear sky was colored a deep shade of blue. The brilliant sun was warm on Ray's skin, lingering like a physical touch. In the warmth of the morning, and before the afternoon heat became uncomfortable, Ray played a rough game of tug-of-war with Harley. The steady, cooling breeze felt good, and would make the day perfect if it lasted.

Ray's stomach quavered in the strange way it always did when he thought about Damien. The feeling was pleasant but weird as hell. It was like Ray was nervous around Damien, when he really was looking forward to it. He enjoyed spending time in Damien's company.

A glance at his watch told Ray that Damien would arrive any moment. Taking his cell phone from the front pocket of his dark blue shorts, he sent a quick text: *In backyard. Come 2 side gate.* Damien's reply was almost immediate: *OK*

Slipping his phone back into his pocket, Ray resumed his two-handed grip on the thick, knotted rope. Ray laughed at the playful growl that accompanied Harley's vigorous headshake. Clamping his jaws tight to the rope, Harley dug all four paws into the grass and leaned back with all of his weight. Ray fought to hold his ground, but Harley was able to drag him forward.

A powerful sounding car parked in the front drive, catching their attention. Harley froze for a moment, the swivel of his ears showing he'd heard the vehicle. The car door closed loudly and Harley dropped the rope, completely forgetting about Ray. He couldn't completely silence his chuckle at Harley's intensity as they both waited for Damien to appear.

Harley's posture was statue-like as he stood staring the side gate. The hair along his shoulders and spine stood straight up, a low growl starting deep in his chest. Ray could relate to Harley's token vigilance, he didn't want to appear too eager either.

"Wanna say 'hi' to Doctor D?" Ray asked, using his higher-pitched, playful tone. "Let's go greet Doctor D!"

Starting toward the sturdy, wrought-iron gate, Harley immediately responded to Ray's relaxed energy and happy voice. Prancing impatiently beside Ray, Harley's aggression turned to excitement, his growl became a whine of anticipation. It was like he was a puppy again; wagging his tail, his tongue hanging from the side of his wide smile. Ray was always happy to see Harley like this, and he laughed openly.

Damien appeared around the corner of the house, the black quarter panel of his flashy Challenger visible behind him. He approached the gate, looking casually handsome in a pair of steel-gray shorts and a sleeveless shirt in a bright shade of blue. That particular blue seemed to surround Damien, and Ray was pretty sure it was his favorite color. Ray's blood warmed at the sight of the rucksack thrown over Damien's shoulder, an overt reminder of his plan to stay the weekend. Sex with Damien was so fucking fantastic; Ray wanted to never get out of bed.

Damien smiled brilliantly when he spotted Harley. "Hello, Harley!" he called, his voice playful. "Hello, boy!" He waited at the gate for Ray to grant him access to *Harley's* territory. Hearing Damien's voice was all Harley needed to become a one-dog welcoming committee. "Hello to you, too," Damien said to Ray, as an afterthought.

"Good morning," Ray called, surprised at how husky his voice sounded. As he returned Damien's smile, Ray's insides quivered like gelatin, his heartbeat fast and flustered.

If Harley remembered that Damien was the evil, mean doctor with the pinchy needles and rectal thermometer, all seemed forgiven now. It even looked like he'd adopted Damien as a member of the family.

That thought stole Ray's breath as he tripped over his own shoe. Harley's easy acceptance of, and affection for, Damien were good things, but it had happened so damn fast. In just a few weeks, Damien had also become a familiar and enjoyable part of Ray's life.

When they neared the gate, Damien unlatched it on his own, proving Ray's hunch that Harley accepted him. Stepping into the yard, Damien greeted Harley with vigorous affection before he resecured the gate. Finally turning his full attention to Ray, Damien lifted his own sunglasses to rest on the top of his head.

"'Morning," Damien said, his voice surprisingly suggestive. He curled his fingers into Ray's tank top, his full lips curving into a small, flirtatious smile. Holding Ray steady, Damien stepped close, the warmth of his body pleasant across the small distance separating them.

Ray lifted his own shades to rest on his head. "'Morning," he whispered, his heart slamming hard against his ribs. Ray held Damien's gaze, trapped by his brilliant blue eyes. He wrapped his own hand over the one Damien had twisted in his pale blue tank top. Leaning forward, Ray covered Damien's mouth with his own. Stepping closer, with a quiet sound of pleasure, Damien encouraged Ray to linger over their kiss. Parting his lips a little, Ray licked lightly at Damien's lips. They parted softly but moved in again with parted lips. Their tongues met lightly, in brief, gentle touches that enticed and teased.

Ray lost himself in his enjoyment of Damien's kiss. His cock stirred with leisurely interest, not impatient or demanding. Ray was dragged rudely back to reality when he and Damien both tottered. He chuckled reflexively as Harley pushed against their lower legs, shoving himself between them impatiently. Damien snorted a laugh, stepping backward but maintaining his grip on Ray's shirt.

"Shame on us." Ray pretended to chastise. "How dare we forget that you're *always* the center of attention?" When he leaned over to give affection, Ray was taken aback when Harley moved away from him.

Damien barked a surprised laugh as Harley seemed to herd him away from Ray. "Uh–oh," he said through his laughter, "somebody's being possessive!"

Ray watched Damien scratch behind Harley's ears, as a powerful surge of affection overwhelmed him for several moments. Harley accepted Ray's family and friends, once they became familiar. But Damien was the first person he'd shown the same type of attachment that he showed toward Ray. Taking a deep breath, he tried to ease the tightness in his chest. As Damien began to straighten up, Ray quickly lowered his shades back over his eyes.

"That's points in your favor, you know," he said, hiding behind a wide smile. "Dogs are excellent judges of character." Ray quickly fisted his hand, hoping to mask how it trembled.

"I'm honored," Damien said playfully. Stepping around Harley, he headed for the house.

Harley took off across the yard at a run. He retrieved his extra-large Kong toy from the grass, carrying it into the shade beneath a lemon tree. The hardened rubber squeaked as Harley happily chomped on it with his powerful jaws. Laying on his belly, eyes half-closed in bliss, he happily gnawed away at his toy.

The inside of the house was still cool and comfortable, even without the AC on, yet. Ray set aside his sunglasses, blinking rapidly as his eyes adjusted to the sudden absence of bright sunlight. "Might as well go put your gear in my bedroom," Ray said with a practiced nonchalance. "Feel free to unpack your toothbrush, and anything else you'll wanna grab quick, later on." He wanted Damien to feel welcomed and comfortable, but not pressured or controlled. It was a fine balance Ray wasn't sure he managed very well.

"That's a great idea," Damien's reply sounded pleased. "I'll go do that. Thank you." His voice faded as he disappeared down the hallway.

Ray smiled inwardly, gratified by Damien's cheerful response. Putting a hazelnut–flavored capsule into the coffeemaker, he pressed the button to brew. In the meantime, he started pulling items out of the refrigerator. Between the two of them, he and Damien made a pretty stellar brunch. Ray considered it was a lot of fun too, even the washing up afterward.

Behind him, Damien scuffed a foot and moved an item on the countertop, telling Ray he'd returned and avoiding surprise. Coming to stand at his back, Damien rested his hands on Ray's hips. "Thank you," Damien said, pressing a kiss to the back of Ray's neck. "So, what's the plan? Our usual for brunch?"

He liked how Damien rested his chin on Ray's shoulder, watching him separate the bacon strips for cooking. "Absolutely," Ray answered, feigning indifference. "Afterward, we'll discuss colonial American literature, then take long naps in separate beds."

Stepping away, Damien burst into laughter. "Screw that!" he said when he'd caught his breath. "Is that coffee I smell?" Damien sounded equal parts reverent and aroused.

Receiving the precise reaction he'd hoped for, Ray smiled in delight. "It's probably ready for you." He pulled a large skillet from the cupboard, setting it atop the stove. Moving to the pantry, Ray began to collect the ingredients to make pancakes.

Damien's voice sounded puzzled when it broke into Ray's thoughts. "I'm only finding hazelnut coffee. Should I check somewhere else?"

Ray glanced up to find Damien looking in the cupboard above the coffeemaker. "Oh," he said sheepishly. "You officially converted me. Just pop in a hazelnut." Damien turned to shoot him a surprised look. Ray returned with a chagrined smile.

Looking affronted, Damien replied, "After all the shit you gave me about drinking wimpy coffee, insisting real men only drink coffee that resembles road tar, and French roast was the only real coffee." Pretending anger and resentment, Damien started the coffee pot brewing again.

Closing the pantry door, Ray said, "Well, I realized you were right."

Damien added some creamer from the fridge to his coffee, while Ray started mixing and cooking. With his coffee mixed to perfection, Damien started to help with brunch. Ray handed him an empty bowl, exchanging it for his cup of coffee. Sharing the same cup was a happy side benefit to drinking the same flavor of coffee. First as a Marine, then as a cop, Ray drank coffee that could pass as jet fuel. He wasn't going to admit to Damien though, how much more he actually *enjoyed* drinking coffee now.

His cozy kitchen had plenty of countertop space, but Damien and Ray could barely make a move without colliding somehow. It made preparing the meal all the more fun. Damien brushed their shoulders together, letting the contact linger. Ray placed a hand on Damien's hip, reaching past him for a utensil. Pressing himself to the length of Damien's back, Ray reached both arms around him. Together, they finished slicing all the fruit and arranging it on a plate.

"I still can't believe you used to serve the syrup cold," Ray mused as they sat down to eat. A gravy boat filled with warm syrup sat in the center of the table.

Damien rolled his eyes, giving a resigned sigh. "I can't believe you didn't know to put vanilla extract in your French toast batter. Your brain was probably clogged by that sludge you call French roast. I'm sensing a pattern."

"No idea what you're talking about," Ray said flatly as he slathered butter on his French toast and pancakes. "I'm making French dip sandwiches for lunch, if you'd like one."

"Sounds good. Am I invited for lunch, then?" Damien gave him a mischievous grin.

Ray chuffed a laugh. He loved Damien's humor, and his playfulness. His intelligence made it energizing to be around him, and his light-heartedness made it fun. "This *is* your complete down weekend, isn't it? That's why you brought your gear, right?" Ray's stomach dropped; for a moment he was afraid Damien was planning to spend some of his coveted down time with someone else.

"I'm only spending today with you," replied Damien, dousing his plate with warm syrup. "I'm spending Sunday with Harley. It's the only way to keep him from getting jealous and taking you back to court to revise the custody agreement."

Ray snorted into his coffee—his own cup this time—wondering if Damien was aware of how close he was to the truth where Harley was concerned. Ray ignored how strongly relieved he was, that Damien was staying and that he really seemed to want to stay. Still laughing, Ray looked over at Damien, impressed that he was managing to keep a straight face. He finally gave in when Ray met his gaze, giving him a wide, brilliant smile.

Between the two of them, they managed to put away a hell of a lot of food. They sat at the table, over the remnants of the meal, swapping stories about their previous weeks at work. Ray was contented; he'd be happy if this moment never ended.

• • • •

RAY SAT IN THE CORNER of the sofa, one foot propped on the ottoman, his other leg extended against the cushions of the back. Damien sat between his legs, reclining against Ray's chest. The lights were dim as they watched a movie that didn't really hold Ray's attention. It was some police action film that didn't approach anything close to realistic. Ray didn't care, though; he just enjoyed having Damien in his arms.

"Does that type of thing even happen in real life?" Damien asked, surprising Ray and pulling him out of his woolgathering.

Ray tuned back in to what was happening on the screen. The lead actor's cop character was in the middle of a very graceful—well choreographed—martial arts fight with a villain. The fight lasted several minutes, both characters were very bloody, but neither was breathing very heavy.

"No," Ray answered languidly. "I don't know anyone who has those kinds of fight skills. I also don't know any drugged-out dirtbag who can stay on his feet that long, let alone with those kinds of skills. And that's who usually tries to resist arrest."

Damien chuckled. "Not to mention the fact that you'd get some help from Harley, if you found yourself in fistfight."

"As long as I can reach the button on my belt that pops his door open," Ray replied without thinking.

First Damien tensed, then he sat up, pausing the movie. He twisted to look at Ray over his shoulder. "What happens if you can't get the door open? Has that ever happened?"

Ray blinked rapidly at Damien, his mind going completely blank. He sensed that a truthful answer might land him in some hot water, but Damien had a talent for knowing when Ray was withholding intel. "When a cover unit gets on scene, the deputy can let Harley out. Not that Harley needs to be released, with another deputy on scene." Damien's expression was thunderous, which left Ray bewildered. "No, it's never happened to me. I can sense when a situation is headed south, so I make sure Harley's in play *before* things get out of control." He hoped his answer placated Damien; Ray didn't want to be the reason he was upset.

"How often do things go south on you?" Damien demanded, eyes narrowed. "Does Harley frequently provide protection for you? Have you ever been injured on the job?"

Ray shifted apprehensively until he had both feet on the floor. Damien fired the questions at him so fast, Ray wasn't sure he had them straight in his head. He had no idea why Damien was so riled up over Ray's job, but he wanted to calm and reassure him. "My job is damn boring, most of the time. They train us on ways to control situations so they never escalate. And Harley makes everybody think twice, just by hanging out the window of my patrol car and barking." Ray smiled, trying to be reassuring, hoping he'd given Damien answers he was looking for.

"If Harley's window is down, can't he get out? Why do you still need to activate the door?" Damien frowned in puzzlement.

"His window is only lowered halfway," Ray answered quickly. "Just enough to get his head and shoulders out, so he can be seen and heard."

Damien studied him for several interminable moments, his expression impassive. Abruptly, he turned so that he could see Ray without having to look over his shoulder. "I believe you that you're not in danger very often. But I think you're downplaying how dangerous things *have* been for you in the past."

Ray considered Damien's words. He'd been in a fuckton more danger, on a daily basis, as a Marine. "I'm a lot safer now than I was as a Marine," he said emphatically. "I used to see combat almost every day, getting shot at with automatic weapons, barely avoiding stepping on or driving over IEDs, taking accurate mortar fire." Ray couldn't bring himself to mention grenades. Still, he didn't miss the quick flick of Damien's eyes toward the ink-covered scar on his forearm. "The worst I've encountered on patrol here is handguns, knives, and baseball bats. Everyone who's taken me on directly, though, used their bare hands."

"Fair enough," Damien replied smoothly. "Is there any time that having Harley made the difference between you getting hurt and going home safe?" Ray thought he saw a hint of a challenge in Damien's eyes.

It was a direct question, so there was no way Ray could evade giving a direct answer. "There was one time, you probably won't like hearing about, but it wasn't as big a deal as it sounds." Despite his disclaimer, he was sure this story would worry Damien. Ray wasn't sure why it mattered, suddenly. "It was late afternoon, just as the sun was starting to go down, and I drove through the parking lot of a small county park on my beat. It's not known to have a lot of criminal activity, but the occasional addict, or group of raucous teenagers will bother the people using the park. I drive through, once or twice a shift, to let myself be seen, and to check for suspicious persons." Damien nodded his understanding. He frowned as he listened, an intense look in his eyes. "I observed a subject exit a group of bushes onto the jogging path. Experience told me he was a drug addict, and I needed to determine if drug deals were being done inside a park where families with children frequently hold parties and play softball. I put my patrol car into park and exited the vehicle, calling out to the subject to initiate a pedestrian stop."

"You left Harley in the car?" Damien asked.

"Yes," Ray answered. "The window was down halfway, so the subject would see and hear him, while he barked. The subject slowed but didn't stop. He scuffed his feet as he walked, denying he was up to anything. I told dispatch where I was and what I was doing, and asked for another unit to start my way, just in case." As he talked, Ray mimed keying his shoulder mic and tilting his head to speak. "I approached cautiously. The guy was unwashed, his hair was grungy, and his clothes were filthy." Damien looked like he had a question, and Ray anticipated what it was. "None of that made him suspicious. His bad skin, rapid eye moment, constant nervous swiveling of his head, and twitchy movements were all signs of chronic heroin use." Damien's single nod and smoothing of his expression told Ray his question had been answered. "I was extra cautious because the weather was warm, and he wore a thick hoodie with his hands in the pockets. If he wasn't hiding drugs, he might have a small weapon." Ray demonstrated the subject's posture, and the position of his hands in the pockets.

"He wouldn't want you to find either one, would he?" Damien's expression was knowing.

Ray was pleased with Damien's intuitive understanding of the situation. It made it easier for Ray to tell the story. He had less to explain, and less to justify. "That's right. So, I ordered him again to stop walking, and to slowly remove his hands from his pockets, so I could see them. He stopped walking but didn't take his hands out." Gesturing in front of his body, Ray showed Damien how everyone was positioned. "I placed myself on the jogging path, blocking the direction he'd been walking. This also gave Harley a straight shot toward the subject *if* I had to deploy him." Damien avidly followed Ray's fingers, understanding the scene setting. "Long story short; this guy got twitchier by the second. When he finally withdrew his hands from his pockets, he had what was basically a miniature toy baseball bat." Lifting his arms, Ray indicated the simple way the weapon had been hidden from his sight. Damien's eyes widened and he seemed to anticipate the direction Ray's story would go. "He'd slid the bat up the sleeve of his hoodie, holding it along his forearm. He cupped the wide end in his hand and hid it in his pocket. As soon as he pulled his hands out, the fight was on."

Damien winced, but still looked worried about the outcome of the story. Again, he glanced quickly at Ray's scarred forearm. "I've never seen a bat like this, before or since. He let it slip down until he held the grip in his hand, and he came at me swinging. Because it was still daylight, I didn't have my Maglite with me." Ray lifted an arm over his head. "He was high on heroin, and he came at me from above, so it wasn't as bad as it could have been. I was able to deflect the blows by reaching for his wrist, his hand, and the grip of the bat. I kept him from landing blows, for the most part, on my arms, shoulders, and head. He changed the direction of his swings and managed to land a blow on the back of my ribcage." Damien gasped, his expression even more worried. "My ballistic vest absorbed a lot of the blow, so nothing was broken, but it stole my breath for a moment."

"Did you have bruised ribs?" asked Damien.

With a shake of his head Ray replied, "No. I was black and blue for a few weeks, but no damage to bone. He connected a glancing blow to my shoulder, which stunned me, so I was slow to deflect the swing at my head."

Damien closed his eyes, his expression pained. "I keep starting to ask you why you didn't do this, or why not try that. I have to remind myself that you're a peace officer. You view threatening situations differently than the rest of us, and you react to them differently. You probably thought the final outcome should be different from what the rest of us thought."

Ray smiled ruefully. "Well, he *did* clock me in the head, so I might not have been thinking clearly at this point." Damien huffed quietly, rolling his eyes. "He hit me hard enough I saw stars, and it knocked me to my knees. I knew I was in trouble, so I popped Harley's door. I don't have a clear memory of the next several moments, but I heard Harley close by, so I knew he'd engaged the subject. He bought me enough time to get my head clear and get to my feet."

"I hope he managed to bite the arm that had ahold of the bat," Damien said darkly. He looked righteously angry and it felt nice, having someone pissed off on Ray's behalf.

"I think that was the first place he bit," Ray said with grim satisfaction that he saw echoed in Damien's expression. "I heard Harley growling and snarling, and this guy was shouting and swearing. I struggled to clear my head so I could get to my feet. I managed to key my mic and tell dispatch I needed my cover unit to respond ASAP, with lights and siren. As I staggered to my feet, I managed to get my asp off my gun belt." Ray paused to question Damien. "Do you know what an asp is?"

"It's a collapsing baton, isn't it?" Damien held up his hands, palms facing each other. He varied the distance between his hands, simulating the action of an asp.

"Exactly," Ray concurred. "So, I got my asp deployed and evaluated the current situation. The guy had dropped the bat, and he'd grabbed Harley by the neck." He held his fists in front of himself. "Normally, that wouldn't faze Harley. But this guy got lucky. He'd gotten hold of Harley's collar and he'd twisted it around his fists. He'd managed to restrict Harley's breathing."

"Oh shit," Damien murmured under his breath. His eyes were wide and he seemed to dread hearing the rest of the story.

"Seeing Harley's body going limp, his eyes roll back in his head, cleared my head immediately." Ray stared blindly into the distance as he remembered. "I wanted this guy to let go of my dog, but I didn't want to kill or cripple him, and have to live with that. So, I used the asp on some of the fleshier, more sensitive parts of his body. I yelled at him to let my dog go, I swore at him, and I left some good bruises. I guess hearing my voice was enough to fire Harley up again. He started fighting back, and between the two of us, we got Harley free."

"Good. That's good," Damien enthused on a relieved sigh. "But how did you get this guy under control?"

"He kept coming at me, even though he'd dropped the bat," Ray answered. "I think he was so high, he didn't know what he was doing. So, I employed different methods of pain compliance, while Harley repeatedly bit into both of his legs." He made gestures with his hands, indicating Harley's snapping jaws. "When my cover unit arrived, the subject seemed to realize he was outnumbered, so he finally gave up. The other deputy cuffed him while I secured Harley."

"How badly were the two of you hurt?" Damien ran his palm up and down the length of Ray's thigh.

It was a comforting touch, and Ray appreciated the gesture. There was a note of vulnerability in Damien's question, though. Ray covered Damien's hand reassuringly with one of his own, still nonplussed by this entire conversation. "Harley and I were each a little beat up, but the guy we arrested was the only one who required medical treatment."

"Good!" Damien declared. "Did you get Harley checked out, just in case?"

"I called the after-hours emergency line when we reached the station." Ray scanned his memory of the timeline. "You were on staff then, but you weren't on call," he said, answering the unspoken question in Damien's eyes. "Harley's energy level and behavior were normal, he ate and drank with his typical enthusiasm, and wasn't sore to the touch. The vet on call told me to bring him in if any of that changed."

"That's reasonable," Damien said amiably. "What about you, though?" he asked dubiously. "You refused to have a doctor check you out, didn't you?"

Ray felt Damien's flirtatious smile right in his gut. He grinned in return. "I let them check me out when I transported the prisoner to the ER to have his numerous dog bite wounds treated."

Damien laughed and the day brightened once again. "Good for Harley! And what did the doctor say about your injuries?"

"Ice, rest, and Ibuprofen!" Ray declared. He lifted Damien's hand, pressing the back of it to his lips. "I transported the prisoner after I completed all the arrest reports, which gave the bruises time to develop, but that just meant the injuries looked worse than they actually were. The best part of all happened back at the station, while we were waiting for all the paperwork. The asshole was secured to the bench where prisoners wait for us to transport them, everyone's adrenaline had come down, and so his mouth was in overdrive. He tried taunting me, mouthing off about how he'd kicked my dog's ass, and how he'd choked my dog out, and how we picked a fight, but he won it. I looked up from my computer and I said, 'You're sitting there in handcuffs, waiting to go to the emergency room where someone will pour peroxide into the open wounds, caused by my dog, which will make them all burn like they're on fucking fire. Afterward, you'll spend the night on an uncomfortable bed in a crowded jail infirmary, suffering through heroin withdrawal. Tomorrow, they'll feed you a meal you're either too sick to eat, or which is so nasty, you'd rather go hungry. My dog, on the other hand, will spend tonight in his own home. He'll stand in his own kitchen and be hand fed his favorite treats. Finally, he's going to sleep in his own big, warm, soft, comfortable bed, in the privacy of his own home. Wanna tell me again who won that fight?'"

Damien threw back his head and laughed, joyfully expressing his delight in Ray's story. His laughter reached his eyes, causing the deep blue color to sparkle. The corners of his eyes crinkled, adding character to his face, making him even more handsome. His sudden curiosity about Ray's job had been strange, but that was in the past now. Relaxing into the sofa once again, Ray tugged Damien down alongside him. He came willingly, resting relaxed and compliant against Ray's chest. He started the movie again, but Ray still didn't pay close attention.

It had been remarkably easy to tell his story to Damien. The judgment and the tension Ray had expected to develop between them never manifested. Having Damien this close made sense; it felt right. Ray kissed his way along Damien's jaw, teasing the corner of his mouth. Damien didn't hesitate to turn into Ray, to join their mouths. Ray even felt his lips curve upward in a smile.

"You're not at all interested in this movie, are you?" Damien asked through a husky laugh.

"Not as much as I'm interested in having you right where you are." Ray placed kisses down the length of Damien's neck.

"Why did you agree to watch it?" A small shiver coursed through Damien's body. "If you were bored, why didn't you say something?"

"Because you wanted to watch it." Ray nuzzled the shell of Damien's ear. "I get every weekend off. This is your only full weekend off this month. You're either on call, on standby, or actually handling emergencies at the clinic."

Damien pulled away and sat up. He turned to look directly at Ray. "Are you serious?" he asked softly, his expression incredulous. "You're willing to do whatever I want to do, all weekend long?" He looked pleased, but still a little hesitant.

Ray wasn't sure why it was so difficult to believe him. "Yeah. You've earned it. You put in long, hard hours some weeks. There may come a time when you can return the favor." The words were out of his mouth before it occurred to Ray he was talking about the future; a long-term future. He tensed, waiting for Damien's response.

A seductive smile spread slowly across Damien's face. "And if I wanted to turn the movie off and spend the rest of the afternoon in bed, would you come with me?"

Ray paused, pretending to consider the question. He snatched the remote from Damien's hand, hitting the power buttons to shut down all the electronics. "What are you waiting for?" Ray demanded, tossing the remote aside. "Get moving! I'm right on your six."

Chapter 7: Who Knew This Day Would Go To Hell?

Looking up from the shift briefing materials, Ray checked his watch. It was 1446 hours, so there was a little time before the actual start of the shift. He went back to ignoring the conversations that filled the room. It looked like his entire shift roster was already present for briefing, which was good because Ray hated having to write anyone up for something as minor as lateness.

Checking his watch again, Ray decided it was time. "Good afternoon, everyone. Let's get started." The room quieted as all the deputies turned to face the front of the room. "Day shift had some excitement today. A traffic stop on a parolee turned into a failure to yield. The pursuit lasted around fifteen minutes until the suspect crashed and bailed. Despite having a canine on scene for a track, the suspect is in the wind. He's known to have been armed in the past, and several of you are likely already familiar with him. The gang detail is trying to locate a subject—Juan Ramos—for questioning in connection with a shooting two nights ago. If you come across him, call for a cover unit and detain him, then contact Detective Seward. Ramos is a known gang member, and like most gang members, he's probably armed." Ray paused to scan the administrative announcements for anything that needed special attention. "Be sure to check your department email for the latest policy and procedure updates. Response is required so don't blow it off too long. We're all adults, don't make me have to hunt you down."

Quiet laughter rippled through the room. Ray kept his expression blank as he scanned the grinning faces of his deputies. He only pretended to be a hard-ass shift sergeant, and he knew they knew that. His time in the Marines meant Ray ran a tight ship and didn't take shit from anybody, but he was approachable and reasonable. Harley helped in that regard, too.

"Okay, listen up for your patrol assignments." The same deputies tended to patrol the same parts of town, so reading off the roster went quickly. "Bronson and I are both on in Vista as your canines tonight. Harley and Ingo are both available for drug searches. San Marcos is short a canine on this shift, but Davies is out there with Baron. And Fallon is on in Fallbrook with Ricco, so we'll work it out if things go tits-up. Any questions?" There were none. "Okay. Let's hit the streets and be safe."

The room exploded with sound as the briefing broke up. As the deputies moved past him, they collected details on wanted subjects and the stolen vehicle Hot Sheet. When the shift was out the door and headed for patrol cars, Ray went to take care of some paperwork before he hit the streets with them.

He removed his handheld radio from his belt, setting it aside. The radio traffic was broadcast throughout the station, so Ray would hear if he was needed to respond for anything. As he sat down at the patrol sergeant's desk, he thought of Damien again. This happened all throughout the day; every day. Everything Ray saw or heard reminded him of something Damien had said or done. These thoughts were pleasant and welcome, heating Ray's blood as his heart tripped and tumbled around in his chest.

The sex between them was mind-melting, but at the same time it was easy and comfortable. That first-time awkwardness had disappeared like a morning mist in the heat of the afternoon. The ways they came together were influenced by their own individual moods, desires, and preferences, instead of any unyielding rules and roles. Still, it wasn't always sex that bombarded Ray's thoughts and memories. Damien was funny, as well as smart, and he actively listened to Ray as much as he talked. All throughout his day, Ray wondered what Damien would think about certain events. He'd begun keeping a mental list of what he wanted to remember to tell Damien.

He was so easily distracted by his own thoughts these days, it took Ray longer than usual to finish up his paperwork. Affixing one final signature, Ray gathered up the paper-clipped stacks and went in search of the LT. The patrol lieutenant was away from his desk, so Ray placed all the paperwork in his inbox to be reviewed and signed. Retrieving his radio and his shades, he headed out the back door to his patrol car.

The rear parking lot was quiet. Ray's car was parked nearby, the engine running and the AC on, while Harley slept in the back. Before he even reached for the door handle, Harley was awake and sitting up in anticipation. Opening the rear door, Ray let Harley out for a quick break, before they both spent the next several hours in the vehicle on patrol.

While Harley sniffed at the fence line, leaving his own scent marker for the other dogs when they came on shift, Ray popped open his trunk to retrieve the canine ballistic vest. When Harley was sniffing more than he was marking, Ray called him over. The olive-colored vest was easy to strap on, and it protected Harley's chest and ribs. *SHERIFF* was boldly emblazoned on the sides, and his badge hung in front of the chest panel, clearly identifying Harley as a police canine. After a quick drink of water, Harley eagerly climbed back into the patrol car.

It was busy for a weeknight. Things picked up as soon as the sun went down, which was typical. Ray cruised through the city, checking on his deputies at traffic stops, and responding with them to some of the more volatile radio calls.

Deputy Bronson responded to a request for a K9 to do a quick drug search, so Ray headed that direction, as well. Ingo hit on several places inside the car, and a routine traffic stop became a major drug bust. As the shift sergeant, Ray supervised the arrests and the evidence collection. His deputies were all experienced veterans, so Ray's help and guidance weren't in high demand.

He was just about to clear from the call when Deputy Brock called for immediate cover. The unit had spotted Juan Ramos, the gang banger from the BOLO. Before Brock could call for a cover unit, Ramos saw the patrol car and rabbited. Now he was on foot, somewhere in the area. He had to be located for the safety of the neighborhood residents. Ray and Bronson both jumped into their patrol cars to respond.

Harley knew something was happening even before Ray hit the lights and siren. He was on his feet in his compartment, pacing and whining, as if telling Ray to drive faster. The volume inside the vehicle made it damn hard to hear radio traffic, so Ray made sure he had a clear view of his MDT.

Several units converged on the area, with more on route when they cleared from their calls. The primary deputy broadcast Ramos' clothing description. The suspect was observed with something in his hand, but no one was able to verify it was a weapon. While Ray was on route, he advised his deputies to assume Ramos was armed and to proceed with extreme caution. After he asked the dispatcher to notify Detective Seward he was needed to respond, Ray ordered some of the deputies toward specific locations, setting up a perimeter. The first two units on scene received info from witnesses that Ramos was hiding out in a backyard. They flushed him out, but lost sight of him again, just as Ray arrived on scene.

Leaving Harley in the patrol car, Ray secured his command of the scene. He verified the perimeter was locked down. There were enough units to secure the immediate scene, while he and Bronson used their dogs to track Ramos to his current hiding place.

Ray secured the long-line to the nylon loop on the back of Harley's vest, and then let him jump down onto the pavement. His ears were forward and he was already pulling hard on the lead. "Heads on swivels, gents," Ray called out to his deputies. "This guy's dangerous." He played out the long-line as Harley picked up their suspect's scent. With Brock on his six, gun drawn to provide cover, Ray leaned back against Harley's pressure on the lead and just tried to keep up with the focused and determined dog.

Now that it was full dark, the air temperature had dropped to a level that could optimistically be called comfortable. The daytime heat, incarcerated in paved surfaces and dark-colored motor vehicles, escaped in a constant exodus that would last another several hours. Tracking in between two houses, Harley led them to a chest-height chain link fence. Broadcasting their updated location, Brock located a gate as Harley paced the fence line, nose still pressed to the ground.

Sweat beaded at Ray's hairline, occasional drops rolling down his face and neck. When his movements shifted his Kevlar vest away from his body, bursts of hot air ghosted over his neck and throat. Ray watched Brock climb easily over the fence. He hefted Harley up into his arms and passed him to Brock over the top of the fence. Harley was capable of clearing obstacles of that height, but Ray refused to risk an injury; he lifted him over whenever possible.

As soon as Ray clambered over the fence, Brock lowered Harley to the ground. With just a few sweeps of his head, he recaptured Ramos' scent and resumed the track. A light breeze gave a little relief from the heat, but only when they were out in the open. Ray quickly grew to hate every alley and patio that Harley led them through. Pulling relentlessly on the long-line, Harley took them over a narrow strip of grass masquerading as a property border between two single-family homes. The lack of a moon helped the grass perpetuate its fraud, but the brittle crunch beneath the soles of Ray's boots gave the game away.

Harley picked up his pace when they entered a backyard of a surprising size. Surrounding houses blocked the streetlamps, as well as porch and patio lights. The landscaping surrounding them loomed menacingly in the mostly-dark yard, the narrow beam of Brock's Maglite barely illuminating small patches of ground and clusters of leaves. The fact they were tracking a gangbanger with a tendency toward violence didn't help Ray's tension level.

Harley was solidly on the track, and sending signals that the scent was strong. He led them toward a thick cluster of foliage beside a rickety wooden shed. Ray had a split second to be thankful his night vision was functioning when he saw movement in the shadows of the bushes. Harley lunged forward aggressively, unleashing his most vicious bark. The shadows shifted as a human shape materialized, wearing dark clothing that matched Ramos' description.

Too fast for Ray to react, the figure scaled the eight-foot fence that stood behind the shed. Harley barked and lunged, eager to be released to make the apprehension. It was too fucking dark for Ray to positively identify the figure as Ramos, so he couldn't send Harley in pursuit. He'd only just begun to shout a warning about the dog, when the shadow disappeared over the top of the fence.

"Fuck!" Ray snarled. Officer safety and public safety were both under threat, ratcheting up Ray's already high-tension level. Brock's flashlight illuminated a gate, so they headed for it. He wanted this guy caught *before* someone got hurt.

Harley darted out as soon as he could fit through the gate, literally towing Ray in his wake. Harley barked again and Ray spotted the shadowy figure at their 9 o'clock, running toward the street. He and Harley pursued, Brock still right on Ray's six. The figure reached the front of the house and darted left, toward the entrance. Ray shouted his warning, eager and ready to release Harley as soon as he knew there was a clear path. Shouts from the street and clipped radio transmissions told him more deputies were responding to provide cover.

Ray reached the front yard just as the suspect kicked in the front door of the house. Brandishing a gun, he stormed into the residence. Distressed shouts and screams reached Ray from inside the house. Shit was deteriorating quickly and Ray was losing control of the scene. He needed to square things away ASAP.

With civilians clearly occupying the residence, Ray couldn't send Harley in. His primary responsibility was the safety of the neighborhood residents. They needed to get Ramos into custody, but not at the expense of innocent citizens.

Pulling back from the entrance of the house, Ray began to collapse the perimeter. He ordered his deputies into specific locations around the house and at strategic places all along the street. The radio crackled to life when his patrol lieutenant advised he was on route to the incident. Ray breathed a quick sigh of relief that he had one less thing weighing on his shoulders. He replaced Harley's long-line with a regular leash, placing the long-line on the hood of a nearby patrol car. Nathan and a few San Marcos deputies were moving in to help cover regular activity in Vista, while they all dealt with what had become a barricaded suspect, so Ray took cover behind the patrol vehicle, and considered his options.

"Please tell me we have a definite ID on this guy!" he shouted, glancing around. "I don't want to find out later on we took down some random dirtbag with a gun, while Juan Ramos slipped away in the dark!"

"I've had multiple previous contacts with Ramos, Sarge," Deputy Lloyd spoke up. "I saw the suspect when he came around the front of the house, and I recognized him as Ramos."

"Good." Now Ray had to figure out how to make contact and get Ramos to release the civilians unharmed. He advised the dispatcher to put SWAT on standby, in case they were needed. Ray looked around at his deputies, taking cover behind strategically parked patrol cars with their weapons drawn. "Remember, we got civilians inside the house, and no idea where. *Do not* fire into the residence until we have more info, or we get them clear of the house."

Keying his shoulder mic, Ray asked Nathan to respond to his location. He advised Nate to pull a few deputies from the neighboring cities to assist with evacuating the residences on the perimeter. Ray was doing his damnedest to bring this to a peaceful conclusion, with no civilian injuries.

Ray was relieved when the LT arrived on scene. Now he had someone to bounce ideas off, someone to verify his ideas were sound. Nathan arrived, tasking a few San Marcos and Fallbrook units with clearing all the houses on the block. Ray felt a hell of a lot better.

He had the car's radio mic in hand, ready to use the PA to get Ramos' attention and start communication. Angry shouts mixed with frightened screams came from inside the house. Everyone tensed, and Harley barked aggressively, when Ramos yanked open the front door. He stood just inside, brandishing a handgun. Ray couldn't quite identify the weapon, but it was a semiauto with a standard magazine, so up to sixteen rounds could be fired in their direction.

Standing in the doorway, Ramos shouted incoherently. There was an agitation to his anger that Ray frequently observed in meth users. That made shit infinitely worse.

"Juan, this is Sergeant Lerner," Ray said through the PA "We just need to talk to you, is all. This has gotten way out of hand."

Ramos shouted a response that Ray couldn't understand. He gestured wildly with the gun. Ray thought he heard women crying inside the house.

"Hey, Juan. All that racket behind you makes it too hard to hear," Ray said, trying to sound conversational. "Who you got in there with you?"

"Man, I got two of 'em in here," Ramos shouted. "These two bitches won't shut up! I can't think with them screechin' like that!"

At least two women inside the house with a gangbanger on meth. This situation was fucked. "Juan, just send 'em out here, so I can get 'em out of the way, and you and me can talk."

"Fuck no!" Ramos shouted angrily. "These bitches is the only thing keeping you assholes from cappin' my ass." He slammed the door closed, rattling the windows of the house.

Ray heard screams and more crying from inside, but it faded quickly. Most importantly, there was no gunfire. That didn't mean Ramos wasn't carrying a knife. Hell, there was probably an entire kitchen full of sharp knives. Ray ran the back of his hand over his forehead, took a deep breath to steady himself, and to get his thoughts under control. The pavement beneath his feet radiated captured heat. Sweating like he was back in the sandbox, Ray shifted in his Kevlar vest. It did little to help, so he just had to ignore his discomfort.

"I'm gonna call out SWAT," the lieutenant said, already putting his cell phone to his ear. "This guy's got a history of violence, and he's unpredictable. You're doing a great job, Ray, but this is SWATs thing."

Ray nodded his understanding. His ego wasn't bothered by handing this goat-roping over to the specialists.

Tension spiked again when the door was abruptly jerked open again. Ramos still had the gun in his hand, waving it wildly. Ray hoped to hell the meth didn't make Ramos' finger twitchy; somebody might get killed by a wild shot.

"I'm not gonna let you assholes kill me!" Ramos shouted so loud, his voice cracked. "I'm not goin' down without taken a bunch of you bastards with me!"

He gestured directly at all of them with the muzzle of the gun.

"Nobody is gonna die here, Juan," Ray said calmly. "All anybody wants is to talk. That's all. Just talk."

"Fuck you!" Ramos blindly fired two shots toward them, in rapid succession.

"Hold your fire!" Ray bellowed, as they all ducked lower behind the patrol cars. He didn't hear any impacts. "Hold your fucking fire! We don't know where in the house he's got those two women!" If one of his deputies got nervous and fired at the house, the chances were good a round would blast through a window and right into one of the female hostages. It was a damn good thing they'd gotten all the neighbors out of their houses, if Ramos kept firing wildly.

Ray glanced over the car hood. Ramos was back inside with the door closed. This was escalating fast. He hoped SWAT got their asses here quick.

Before Ray could decide his next move, the door opened again. The only thing illuminated by the porch light was Ramos' hand wrapped around the gun. He fired twice, keeping them all behind cover.

"You want these bitches? Fine. Take 'em!" An elderly woman appeared in the doorway, her terror obvious even in the dim light of the porch. She stumbled onto the porch like she'd been pushed, almost losing her balance. She struggled to make it down the three small steps without falling. Next, a middle-aged woman stumbled out onto the porch. She quickly made it down the steps, helping the elderly woman down the last one.

The entire house shook on its foundation when Ramos slammed the door.

"Go get 'em!" Ray ordered, gesturing for several nearby deputies to move forward. "Get 'em to where the FD is staging, so medics can check 'em out."

Two deputies moved into the yard. Two more accompanied them, weapons drawn and pointed toward the house. Reaching the women, the first two deputies placed themselves between the house and the women's backs. Under cover provided by the second two deputies, they supported the frightened women, moving them quickly out of the line of fire.

"Is Seward on scene?" Ray shouted. He looked around, trying to spot the gang detective.

Brian Seward moved forward, joining Ray and the LT behind the patrol car. He was about Ray's age, sporting a scraggly beard. He wore his shirt buttoned to the throat, and his jeans nearly falling off, just like the local gangbangers he worked with.

"Some clusterfuck, huh?" Brian asked mirthlessly. "Ramos is a violent hothead, and we know he's almost always armed. He's never been this out-of-control, though."

"He's got the manic, jittery look of a meth-head," said Ray.

Brian rolled his eyes. "He's known to use, but I've never had contact with him when he was this jacked-up."

"All you needed was to talk to him?" asked Ray, looking for some explanation for this insanity.

"I need to talk to him 'cause he's a suspect in a one-eighty-seven," Brian said darkly. "But I wasn't spreading that around, for this reason!"

"Christ," Ray muttered, shaking his head.

The door opened and three shots rang out over their heads. This time, several deputies returned fire. When the roar of gunfire faded, Ramos' unhinged laughter reached them.

"You want me, fuckers? You gotta come get me!" The doorway and the interior of the house stayed dark. Ray couldn't see Ramos, or any movement inside. "Come in here and face me, if you wanna talk! Or are you a bunch of pussies?" There were sounds of gunfire and breaking glass from inside the house. Ramos' voice grew faint, as he receded deeper into the residence.

"Somebody get verification from those two ladies that no one else is in there with Ramos!" Ray shouted. He stood up slowly, watching the front of the house from over the roof of the patrol car. He listened to the radio traffic as someone questioned the women, while they were being tended to by medics. They'd been inside the house when Ramos had kicked his way inside. With them out and safe, he was alone inside.

There was gunfire from deep inside the house, three shots this time. One of the deputies holding the perimeter behind the house came up on the radio. "We got rounds coming out the windows back here."

Shit. Ray needed to shut this down, before deputies or bystanders ended up hurt. Or worse.

"We're gonna make entry," he announced. "In through the front and rear doors, simultaneously, and I'll send Harley in to clear the house."

"Come on, you fuckers!" Ramos' voice was slightly louder, as if he'd moved toward the door just to taunt them. "You want me? You wanna talk? You come in and get me, and we'll talk!" Two more gunshots, and more shattered glass. Ramos had fired fourteen rounds. He was nearing empty.

Ray hoped to hell this asshole wasn't carrying another magazine.

"That's risky, Ray," the lieutenant said. "Even sending Harley in first, you're *all* still in a lot of danger."

Ray was well aware. His stomach twisted, turning sour at the thought of sending Harley in after a meth-head with a loaded gun. "LT, we got serious public safety issues here." Implied in Ray's words was the fact that they, as law enforcement officers, were obligated to risk themselves to protect civilians. Harley's training was designed to utilize his strengths to protect deputies. "I don't like my own idea. But he's gotta be stopped, and it's too dangerous to wait for SWAT."

Ramos' deranged shouts grew louder, then faded away again.

"All right, Sergeant." The LT's reluctance was obvious, and Ray appreciated that his CO wasn't cavalier about risking lives, including Harley's. "I'll coordinate the entry. Front and back doors, simultaneously. Everyone cover Harley, as he hopefully intimidates this prick into surrendering with minimal resistance."

"Yes, sir," Ray replied. He put his arms around Harley's neck, seeking comfort and reassurance. Harley was too caught up in the excitement, he refused to sit still and tolerate Ray's confinement. His high energy, his enthusiasm was essential in a police K9, and what made Harley such a damn good one.

Nathan appeared, called forward by the lieutenant to help coordinate the perimeter units while Ray made entry. The team of deputies the LT assigned to go in as cover for Harley and Ray assembled behind the front fenders of the patrol cars. The team going in the back door radioed the LT that they were in place and ready.

Ray gave Harley the command to bark, hoping to maximize the intimidation factor. He just hoped like hell it worked. He led the deputies toward the house, keeping to the hinged side of the door so they weren't all sitting targets.

At the porch steps, Ray paused to make his announcement. "Sheriff's Department with a canine! Come out now, with your hands above your head, or I'll release the dog and he will bite!"

Two gunshots came from deep inside the house. "Fuck you and your fucking dog! You want me? You gotta come in here and take me yourself!" A fresh wave of adrenaline flooded Ray's system. The porch light seemed brighter, Harley's barking seemed louder. Ray's heart pounded in his chest so hard, it reverberated through the plates of his vest. Ramos was probably out of ammo. If Ray had any luck, or good karma, the asshole didn't have another magazine to reload.

"Last chance to come out, hands on your head! If you refuse, I'll release the dog and you will be bitten!"

"Fuck you!" Ramos' shout wasn't accompanied by gunfire. Ray decided that as a good sign.

Gripping Harley's harness with one hand, Ray unclipped his leash with the other, tossing it to the ground. He pulled his weapon from the holster, ready to follow Harley into the darkness of the house.

To the deputies with him, Ray said, "Sending the dog."

With the command for Harley to locate and apprehend the suspect, Ray let go of his harness.

Chapter 8: When Your Worst Nightmare Becomes Reality

Harley disappeared into the dark interior of the house. Ray held his Maglite in one hand, bracing his gun hand on top of that wrist. He bypassed the steps, climbing right up onto the porch. Stepping quickly through the door, he trained his light on the floor, while those behind him illuminated their surroundings.

The beam of Ray's Maglite swept over pale walls, white trim nearly glowing. The rooms seemed filled with furniture, casting shadowy images on the light carpet. Every flat surface held sprawling houseplants or knickknacks. The house seemed clean and tidy, no easy hiding places, no clutter on the floor that might cause him to trip. The air was cooler in here, with the fresh smell of the outdoors that meant open windows and a cross breeze. Despite that, Ray was still sweating through his skivvy shirt.

Sounds came from the back of the house. Ray was confident it was Harley, methodically searching each room. Catching sight of a flashlight beam in the kitchen moving their way, Ray aimed his weapon in that direction.

"Sergeant Lerner?" a faceless deputy asked just above a whisper.

"Right here," Ray replied, as the second team joined up with them as planned.

"Basement, kitchen, and dining room are all clear."

"Roger that." Ray led the way down the narrow hallway, following the faint sounds coming from the darkened bedrooms.

The darkness erupted with the startling sounds of Harley's barking. Ramos shouted. His rage-filled curses quickly turned to screams. Ray nearly sprinted down the final length of hallway, following Harley's vicious growls, mingling with Ramos' pain-filled screams of fear.

Stepping into the last bedroom, Ray pointed his Maglite in the direction of the ruckus. Harley had Ramos pinned to the floor, his jaws gripping relentlessly at soft flesh. Ramos gripped something in his hand, Ray assumed was his empty firearm. He struck Harley in the side several times with the empty handgun. The blows connected on the side of the ballistic vest, but a couple seemed to land low on Harley's flank.

"Stop fighting him and empty your hands!" Ray shouted, aiming his weapon at Ramos. The other deputies arrayed themselves behind him, all Maglite beams focused on the battle. "Stop fighting him, empty your hands, and he'll stop biting!" Now Ray could see that Harley had bitten Ramos' arm at an angle with such force, he'd also managed to get his teeth into chest muscle. Each shake of Harley's head had to be excruciating—no wonder Ramos was screaming.

Finally, finally stopped striking Harley, dropping what he held in his hand. Ray holstered his weapon, stepping forward to call Harley off of the bite. The deputies behind him shouted orders for Ramos to keep his hands where they could see them.

Just as Ray ordered Harley to release the bite, his light moved over the object Ramos had dropped. His stomach twisted sickeningly, his heart leaping into his throat. After eight years in the Marines, Ray knew the weapon on sight.

"Jesus Christ!" Ray blurted, reaching for Harley as he attached the foot-long loop leash. "Ramos had a knife." Using his flashlight, Ray quickly scanned Harley for any wounds as he started to lead him out of the room. The world around him spun. It was hard to breathe, Ray struggled to get enough air into his lungs.

"Is Harley okay?" someone asked.

"Don't know," Ray said quickly, reaching the hallway. "Can't tell yet." An echo of pain stabbed at his arm, beneath the intricate tattoo.

Ray headed for the front door. The sounds of Ramos being handcuffed faded behind them. Harley kept pace with Ray as they crossed the living room, but his usual exuberance was gone. Ray's blood chilled. He told himself history was not repeating itself; Harley might just be fatigued from all the activity.

As he reached the door, he heard one of the deputies in the bedroom broadcast that they were Code 4, with the suspect in custody. He added that Ray was on route the front yard, and Harley was possibly injured.

Ray swallowed back bile, the sound of the words making the possibility real. Reaching the front porch, he began to check Harley's condition. He used the faint illumination of the porch light, as well as his own Maglite. He was only vaguely aware of the controlled chaos in the yard and the street. Nathan and the LT quickly joined Ray on the porch.

Ray's heart hammered so hard, he heard it thundering in his ears.

Struggling to breathe, he held his mouth wide open, audibly sucking in desperate breaths. Harley sat down, his head hanging low on his neck. He panted heavily, his eyes glazing over. Even as Ray watched, Harley became unsteady, weaving slightly in his sitting position. His greatest fear was happening before his eyes.

"How is he, Ray?" Nathan asked, his voice filled with concern, and a hint of righteous anger.

Shaking his head, more in denial, than a negative answer, Ray took in the sight of blood pooling on the porch. The cuts on Harley's head looked superficial—at least he hoped they were—but the gash in his side, just below the edge of his ballistic vest, was bad—very bad.

"Ramos had a knife," Ray blurted, dropping to his knees. "Harley's lost a lot of blood." There was something he should do, but his brain was locked onto a memory and frozen in place.

The LT didn't hesitate. "Sergeant Santiago, let's get him some help." He took control of the deputies securing Ramos, ordering everyone to provide Nathan with any assistance he needed.

Harley collapsed over onto his uninjured side. The gash in his lower flank was long. Ray couldn't tell how deep it was, but the amount of blood Harley continued to lose meant it wasn't shallow. He was helpless. He hated and dreaded being helpless.

Nathan issued orders to the deputies collected outside the residence as he quickly stripped off Harley's ballistic vest. "Everybody empty your vehicles of towels, T-shirts, anything that'll soak up blood to help stop the bleeding." Deputies sprang into motion, running toward their patrol cars. "Jennings, you help the sergeant with Harley. Tran, we'll load them into the back of your patrol car. I'm authorizing you to roll code to get Harley to the hospital."

The confidence in Nathan's firm voice sliced through Ray's thoughts. He covered Harley's wound with shaking hands. He could at least slow the bleeding until he could get to Damien. "Come on, Harley, buddy." Ray had to get Harley to Damien. He was sure Damien could fix this. He'd make sure Ray didn't lose Harley, too. "Stay with me, Harley. You're gonna be just fine, buddy. Just fine."

Harley tried to wag his tail, but he barely managed to lift the very end from the ground. Ray's vision blurred as warm tears flooded his eyes.

Suddenly, he was surrounded by people and fleetingly, he felt like he was back on the helo. Several towels were pushed into his hands, and against the long wound in Harley's belly. Ray snapped back to the present. Nathan knelt directly across from him, firmly pressing a towel to the wound beside the towel Ray held.

"The back doors of my vehicle are open," said Deputy Tran, handing Ray a fresh towel to replace the one saturated with Harley's blood. "Ready when you are, Sergeant."

"You wanna carry him, while I put pressure on the wound?" Nathan asked. "Or you want me to carry him?"

"I'll get him," Ray replied, swallowing back a sob.

Ray muscled Harley up, nearly onto his belly. His heart broke when Harley yelped in pain, whining pitifully. Ray pressed his dog to his chest and staggered to his feet. Nathan was right there in front of him, pressing a thick towel to the wound.

"This way," Tran said, arms full of clean towels and T-shirts.

Walking as quickly as he could, weighed down by Harley's mass, they made their way to Tran's patrol car. Ray vaguely realized why Nathan had picked Tran for this task, when he saw the vehicle was parked completely clear of all the others stacked up in the street.

"Lay him down on the backseat," Nathan said quietly. "You sit next to his head, Jennings, you sit by his tail, and you both apply pressure."

Ray quickly agreed. He was in no condition to think about logistics or tactics. He was grateful Nathan had that covered. Someone had thought to lay out a blanket. Given the amount of blood, that was a good idea. As gingerly as he could, Ray placed Harley on the backseat of the patrol car. He gasped at the sound of Harley's yelps and whimpers.

"I know. I'm sorry, boy," Ray crooned. "Just hang in there for me. Please, Harley." He crawled in, sat down, and placed Harley's head in his lap. Jennings climbed in the other door. Together, they pressed towels to the still-bleeding wound.

Nathan leaned in, putting a stack of towels and shirts on the floorboard between Ray and Jennings. "Wrap the blanket around him," he said, just before he closed the car door. "He's probably in shock, and that'll keep him warm."

Ray was touched when he realized the blanket hadn't been laid out for the blood, but for Harley's well-being.

All the doors were shut. Nathan's voice was muffled as he and Tran had a brief discussion. Ray wanted to shout at them to hurry up, valuable seconds were being lost that could mean Harley's life. The driver's door was yanked open, and Tran slid behind the wheel. He hit the switch for the lights, illuminated the world outside in yellow, blue, and red. "Sergeant Santiago told me to get you to the North Coast Animal Hospital, sir. I actually know right where that is. The sergeant's going to call ahead to let them know we're on our way."

Ray had to think. He knew he had to get Harley to Damien. He tossed the saturated towel onto the floor, firmly pressing a fresh one to the wound. With his other hand, Ray caressed Harley's head, carefully avoiding the gashes on the side of his face. "Come on, buddy," he murmured softly. "Stay with me, bud. You're gonna be okay." The lights and siren cleared the road in front of them, and Tran pushed the Crown Vic to its upper limits. Ray just hoped it was fast enough to get Harley to Damien in time. "Damien," Ray suddenly blurted, realizing it was after hours. He didn't trust anyone else to save Harley's life. "Doctor Federov," he called to Tran. "I need Doctor Federov. It has to be Damien Federov."

"Don't worry, I got it." Tran slipped his Bluetooth onto his ear. His voice was barely audible over the sound of the siren as he talked to whoever had answered. "Hey, it's Deputy Tran...Lerner says he needs a specific veterinarian when we get to the hospital...good, I'll let him know... less than five minutes...got it...understood." Hitting the button on his Bluetooth, Tran said to Ray, "Sergeant Santiago said Doctor Federov is the vet on duty tonight. He's already there waiting for us to arrive."

"Thank you," Ray said gratefully. He should have known Nathan would have that covered. It was a little easier to breathe now, knowing Damien was there, ready to help. Both towels were soaked through with blood, so Jennings and Ray each swapped for a new one.

Tran left the freeway, never slowing down. He blew through all the lights and hit the hospital parking lot at full speed. "They're supposed to meet us at the back entrance," Tran said as he started to drive around the end of the building.

Damien was waiting for them. He and Luisa had the rear door propped open. Between them was a large rolling cart, heavily padded with blankets. Damien looked so strong and confident; Ray allowed himself a moment of belief that Harley would be okay.

They came to a hard stop and Damien was already in motion. The door behind Jennings opened and he quickly climbed out. Damien leaned in, effortlessly gathering Harley into his arms. Before Ray could get himself moving, Damien had Harley laid out on the padded cart and he and Luisa were wheeling him into the hospital.

Gathering his wits, Ray leapt out of the vehicle to follow the cart bearing his dog. Tran and Jennings flanked him, as Ray charged into the hospital. He froze in mid-step at the sight before him. Harley was laid out on a tall table as Damien, Luisa, and two other staff, all dressed in dark red scrubs, frantically worked. Damien gave orders from where he was bent over Harley's limp form, his hair covered by a brightly patterned surgical cap. He held Harley's unresisting head with both hands, using his thumbs to open both eyelids. Opening Harley's mouth, Damien examined his tongue and gums.

Luisa hung fluid bags from a tall pole, attaching their tubing to the needle she'd inserted into Harley's foreleg. She added another bag of fluid as Damien instructed. Someone slid an oxygen mask over Harley's muzzle. Ray was beside the table before he realized it. Reaching for Harley's head, he held the mask steady with one hand, stroking the thick fur on Harley's neck with the other.

"Ray," Damien said firmly, jolting Ray. "Do you know what Harley was stabbed with?" He examined the long wound with latex gloved hands.

"A Ka-Bar," he replied immediately, remembering that moment of pained recognition.

"Is that a knife of some kind?" Damien's brows knit together in confusion.

"It's a military knife," Ray answered mechanically. "Seven-inch blade, serrated near the hilt."

"Do you know if the blade penetrated fully?"

"No." Ray realized that meant the wound might not be as deep as it seemed.

"How long ago?"

Ray stood mute. He had no idea what time they'd made entry into the house. He had no idea what time it was now.

"Fifteen minutes, tops," Jennings replied.

"Did you start applying pressure immediately?"

"Within two to three minutes," Jennings answered again.

"Good. Very good," Damien said with a nod. He requested a medication that Ray didn't recognize. Luisa injected it into Harley's IV. "Call Doctor Reese. Tell him I need him to come in for a surgical assist."

Ray must have made some sort of distressed sound because Tran and Jennings were suddenly both beside him. They tried to reassure him that it was okay; the vet had everything under control. Ray hadn't been ready for Harley to need surgery. He'd thought Damien would stop the bleeding, stitch him up, replace some of the blood he'd lost, and Harley would be good as new. Christ, surgery meant things were even worse than he'd thought. Ray absently rubbed at his forearm tattoo.

Luisa disappeared through a door across the room. The other two scrub-clad staff raced around, gathering different types of bandages and tools. They filled a rolling tray with implements and stacks of bandages while Damien used his stethoscope to listen to Harley's chest, positioning the tray within Damien's easy reach.

Harley's eyes were half open and still glazed. His chest moved up and down rapidly, each breath shallow. Ray used both hands to stroke Harley's neck. Damien slung his stethoscope around his neck, reaching for the thick gauze covering Harley's wound. The large white square was saturated red. Ray swallowed hard. Damien placed another bandage over the gash, holding it in place.

Luisa reappeared. "Doctor Reese is on his way. He was home, so it'll just be a couple of minutes."

"Good," Damien replied. Reaching up, he grabbed a handle on the large lamp, adjusting the angle of the multi-jointed arm until it shined directly on Harley's flank. "We need to stop the bleeding and prep him for surgery."

Luisa slid latex gloves onto her hands. One of the other techs came to lean over Harley's head, a bottle and a square of gauze in his hands. The stitching on his scrubs said his name was Tony. Luisa handed Damien a stainless steel instrument. Tony began to clean the cuts on Harley's head and face.

"These aren't bad at all," Tony murmured. "Very shallow. Doctor D will only have to throw a couple of stitches in them."

Ray nodded sharply. He knew Tony was trying to be reassuring, but those shallow wounds had never worried him. They'd stopped bleeding right away.

He still appreciated Tony's concern for him, though.

"Ray, I need you to keep Harley steady for me," Damien said, snaring Ray's attention again. "If he wakes up a little, secure his head, just like you usually do. Okay?"

"Yeah, I got it," Ray answered, his voice raw sounding. He looked back down at Harley, stroking his head and neck, looking for signs he might be waking up.

Luisa pushed gauze pads into Damien's hand. He pressed pad after pad of gauze into the large wound. When he pulled them out, they were saturated red with blood. Luisa handed stainless steel instruments to Damien. He reached them into the wound, gently moving them around. Each time he positioned the tool to his satisfaction, he accepted another one from Luisa.

"Got it," Damien said firmly to Luisa. "I'm just gonna stitch this one to stop the bleeding, then we'll prep him for the surgery."

Luisa clipped a long handled instrument to a curved needle, threaded with black string. Handing it to Damien, he used it to close something inside Harley's wound. He quickly applied three stitches. Withdrawing his hands, Damien stripped off his bloody gloves. He used his stethoscope to listen to Harley's chest, and his belly.

With a single nod, Damien glanced at Tony. "Let's apply a pressure bandage, just to hold him until we're in surgery."

Luisa opened a door behind Damien, flicking on the lights. Ray saw a surgical suite, filled with high tech machines. She began turning things on and setting up the room.

With thick pads of gauze covering Harley's wound, Damien began to wrap a bright colored self-adhering bandage around his body. Tony carefully lifted Harley's hips, as Damien passed the roll of bandage underneath. When the white gauze was covered, Damien cut the bandage, pressing the end down to secure it.

Stripping off his fresh latex gloves, Damien looked up and met Ray's eyes. He came around the end of the table, his arm extended to guide Ray away. "Okay, let's go get you guys settled in somewhere comfortable."

Ray resisted, curling his fingers into Harley's thick fur.

"Come on, Ray," Damien said quietly, gently grasping Ray's arm and tugging. "This is going to take a while. You need to get comfortable for the wait, or you won't be any good to Harley when he needs you."

Ray nodded, finally letting Damien steer him away from Harley's frighteningly still form. Tran and Jennings were behind them, talking to Damien as they followed. Ray didn't hear what they said; his mind was filled with images of Harley and all the lost blood. He allowed himself to be guided by Damien's hand on his back toward another closed door.

Chapter 9: It Was Going To Be A Very Long Night

When Damien opened the door, Ray saw they were behind the large reception desk. Damien ushered them into the spacious waiting room. He pressed a light switch on the wall beside the door, illuminating the front half of the room.

"Deputy Tran, you'll want to pull your car around to the front parking lot," Damien said, crossing to the outside door. "You'll also want to keep this locked, so you're not having to deal with stragglers, and the curious. We triage the emergencies by telephone, and control access through various doors. I'm sure more of you guys are going to show up to check on Ray and Harley, so you can direct them to the front entrance, and lock the door again once you let them in."

Jennings was reading his cell phone. "Yeah, they're already demanding updates. Some of the off duty canine handlers want to come give Ray their support."

"Good, I was hoping they would." Damien gestured toward the far side of the room. "We've got the vending machines for you to use. At the very least, you need to stay hydrated, Ray. If someone can bring you real food, you need to try to eat. I know you don't feel like it, but you need to stay strong for Harley."

Ray nodded his understanding. He doubted he could choke down anything, though. He wanted Damien to tell him what was going on. He needed Damien to tell him that Harley would be okay—that everything would be okay.

"You can use the bathroom to get cleaned up." Damien gestured toward the closed door, marked with the usual stick figures. "I'll send Tony out with a bunch of real towels. Is there a way for someone to bring Ray a change of clothes?" he asked Jennings and Tran.

Once Ray could take off his gun belt and get out of his ballistic vest, he'd be a hell of a lot more comfortable. "I don't need to change," he said in a hoarse voice. He reached for the buckle on his tactical belt. When he brushed his hands against his uniform blouse it felt different. Looking down, Ray was shocked by what he saw. His hands were covered in dark, dried blood, caked beneath his fingernails and flaking around his knuckles. His uniform was soaked through, stained from his chest to his knees. "Shit," he blurted, biting back a sob.

"We'll get somebody to bring a T-shirt and sweats, Ray," Tran said. "You can clean up, and you'll feel better."

He couldn't wait. Ray yanked his blouse out of his pants. With a trembling hand, he reached for the zipper hidden behind the panel with faux buttons. Ray jerked the zipper down, trying to strip off his blouse. He got it over his shoulders and down his arms. Jennings was suddenly there, taking the blood-stained khaki from Ray.

It didn't help. The blood had soaked through to his vest. Ray desperately grasped at the Velcro shoulder straps, but he got himself tangled up. Tran stepped up, easily tugging the Velcro free. He removed both panels of Ray's vest and stepped back.

The sight of his pristine white skivvy shirt was a relief. Ray breathed easier. His olive uniform pants were stained, but he could deal with that for a little while. Now it was easy to get his gun belt off, dropping it into one of the waiting room chairs. Kneeling down, he unfastened the ankle holster holding his backup weapon, setting it with his belt. Getting to his feet, he realized he still needed to wash his hands.

Ray took a deep breath. "There's a bag in the trunk of my patrol car that has a full change of clothes." He always carried a change of clothes because he never knew what he might run—or fall—into. "If someone could bring that over?"

Tran immediately put his cell phone to his ear. Ray's vest and blouse had discreetly disappeared, to his relief.

"Okay, let's come over here and talk," Damien said, gesturing toward a pair of chairs tucked into a corner. Ray followed robotically.

They both sat on the edges of their chairs. Ray's leg bounced violently, and he couldn't control it. He clenched and unclenched his hands, searching Damien's face for some sign that Harley would be okay.

"How bad is he?" Ray asked abruptly. He swallowed hard against his tight throat.

"I got the bleeding under control, and I stabilized him," Damien replied quietly. He met Ray's eyes with his own intense gaze. "I won't know the full extent of his injuries until I get him into surgery. I have to repair the severed blood vessels, and check for damage to his internal organs. If something inside was nicked or cut, I have to repair that, too."

"Christ," Ray whispered. He scrubbed a hand over his close-cropped hair, ignoring the blood he still needed to wash off.

Damien put a hand on Ray's knee. "Hey, Ray, listen to me," he whispered. When Ray looked up, he found Damien leaning toward him, meeting his gaze directly. "You know I'm going to do my damnedest to make sure Harley's okay, right?"

"That's the one thing I *am* sure of," Ray replied in a whisper of his own.

"Good." Damien sat up straight. He looked as determined as he did capable. "This could take a while, depending on what I find when I get in there. I'll send Tony out as soon as I know anything for sure. But I need you to be patient." He rose to his feet.

Ray also stood. "I'll try." He took a step closer to Damien, dropping his voice into a whisper again. "I'm not ready to lose him." Ray couldn't meet his eyes while he made his confession. He rubbed absently at the large scar on his forearm.

Damien used both hands to give Ray's shoulders a firm squeeze. "Roger that," he said softly. He called something to Jennings and Tran, and then disappeared back into the depths of the hospital.

"Sergeant Santiago is arranging for someone to drive your patrol car over. He'll be over as soon as they're finished clearing the scene," Tran said into the sudden silence of the waiting room. "A few other handlers are on the way, just to be here for support." Ray nodded. His fellow handlers would understand how he was feeling, how worried he was. "Is there anything you need, man? Anything we can do to help, while we wait?"

"No. I'm fine for now," Ray replied distractedly. "I just don't know how I'm going to make it through the waiting, until I know Harley's going to be okay." Maybe if he said those words often enough, it would make them true.

"We'll take it minute by minute," Jennings said, a comforting hand on Ray's shoulder.

"I'm gonna go bring my vehicle around," Tran said, heading for the exit. "I'll leave this unlocked, so I can get back in."

Ray remembered how they'd practically abandoned Tran's patrol car when they'd arrived. It struck him that he owed Jennings and Tran a great debt.

"Thank you both for your help," he said, feeling awkward. He wished he'd said something to them earlier. "I appreciate what you did for Harley. It means a lot."

"Don't mention it," Tran replied. "Happy to do it." He disappeared out the door to retrieve his vehicle.

Tony appeared in the door behind the reception desk. His arms were full of thick, assorted bright jewel-colored towels. He set them on the tall counter. "Is there anything else I can do for you guys?" he asked, looking eager to help.

"No," Ray answered, sighing heavily. "Not for now. Thanks, man."

Jennings grabbed several towels. "Let's get you cleaned up a little, Sarge."

Ray washed his hands vigorously, lathering up his arms to his elbows. Jennings wet the corner of a towel, and they used it to scrub at Ray's fingernails. Glancing in the mirror, Ray saw small smears of blood on this face and neck. He wet another corner of the towel and rubbed his skin harshly until he felt almost clean. Cupping water in both hands, Ray splashed it onto his face. The coolness felt good.

Shutting off the water, he took the second towel Jennings offered to him. Ray dried his face, neck, arms, and hands. He started to feel a little better, but his stomach was still sick from worry.

When Ray exited the bathroom, Tran was back. He'd put Ray's gun belt on the countertop, beside the towels. "Here." Tran handed him an unopened bottle of water. "Doc says you gotta stay hydrated."

Reluctantly, Ray took the water with a quiet word of thanks. He sipped at it, his stomach protesting. He sat down heavily in one of the chairs, wondering how the hell he was going to keep his sanity while he waited to hear if Harley would live or die. Ray reminded himself that Harley was in Damien's care, and everything would be okay.

Tran suddenly stood, going to unlock the door. A couple of Ray's fellow handlers stepped inside. He greeted them with strong hugs, and they slapped each other's backs vigorously. He filled them in on what Damien had said about the surgery.

Ryan, a K9 handler out of Fallbrook, plunked a bunch of coins into the vending machines. He returned with a candy bar and a can of soda. "Here, you need these. You know adrenaline burns through blood sugar. You're probably crashing. These will balance you out."

Ray took the items, knowing Ryan was right. He wasn't sure he'd be able to choke anything down, but Damien had been right, he had to try to—for Harley. He opened the soda can and swallowed several mouthfuls. Setting it on magazine table beside his chair, Ray tore open the candy wrapper with his trembling hands.

The sweetness tasted dry and flat to him, but he choked it down. He stared at the brightly colored artwork on his forearm, telling himself things were different this time. The single knife did far less damage than an exploding grenade. He'd gotten Harley into Damien's capable care quickly, there'd been no excruciating wait for a helo to arrive.

Ray washed down the candy bar with the last of the soda. The empty can disappeared from his hand. Ryan had been right, Ray felt just a little bit better. Bracing his elbows on his knees, he pressed his fingers into his eyes. Maybe the knife hadn't penetrated very deep. Maybe Damien only had to repair the blood vessels, and stitch the wound closed. He concentrated on his breathing, struggling to keep it slow and steady.

He was vaguely aware of the main door opening briefly and closing again. There were quiet murmurs. A warm, heavy hand came to rest on Ray's shoulder.

"Hey there, buddy," Nathan said from beside him.

Relief washed over Ray, driving him to his feet. Nathan moved in front of him, drawing Ray into a fierce hug. Ray felt compassion and sympathy radiating from his friend. His fellow handlers understood the strength of the bond between a handler and his canine, but Nathan knew exactly what was going on inside Ray's head right now.

"Thanks for coming," Ray murmured against Nathan's shoulder.

"I wouldn't be anywhere else," Nathan replied. He pulled back, gripping Ray's arms. "I brought your patrol car over. And I retrieved your bag from the trunk. It'll help for you to finish getting cleaned up."

Ray nodded, numb and unresisting as Nathan guided him toward the bathroom. He hated the stiff feel of the dried blood on his uniform pants, scratching the bare skin of his thighs. It was uncomfortable enough, but the constant reminder that Harley was hurt made it worse. Nathan ushered him back into the bathroom, closing the door behind them.

The room wasn't spacious, but it was large enough that two full-grown men weren't stepping on each other. Nathan placed the towels on top of the sink and set Ray's rucksack beside the commode. Ray stared blankly at the towels.

Glancing down at his ruck, he had no idea what to do next. He looked back at the towels, unsure if that's where he should start.

"Why don't you take off your boots first," Nathan said softly, leaning back against the door. "Then get out of that T-shirt that reeks of Kevlar."

"Okay," Ray replied dully. It seemed as good a place as any to start. He tugged at the laces of his Hi-Tec boots, toeing each of them off. He tucked his socks inside his boots. Ray's fingers were stiff, refusing to cooperate and follow his instructions. Finally, he managed to get a grip on the hem of his skivvy shirt and pull it up over his head.

"If you wash your face before you put on your fresh shirt, you won't get it all wet," Nathan said conversationally. He took one of the towels, wetting it in the sink. "Here you go." He gestured for Ray to step up to the sink.

Ray complied, even though he didn't see the point. It wasn't worth arguing with Nathan. Stepping to the sink, Ray glanced up at his reflection in the mirror. He froze, knowing the face he saw was his own, but still not recognizing himself. His eyes were wide open, and he looked haunted. It was late enough that his face was shadowed by his new beard growth. Worst of all, there were several smears and smudges of blood on his chin and cheeks.

Grabbing both faucet handles, Ray turned them on full blast. He splashed several handfuls of water on his face. He ran his damp palms over his scalp. Shutting off the water, Ray braced himself on the edges of the sink, breathing heavily.

"You okay?" Nathan asked in a cautious tone.

He wasn't really, and he wouldn't be until Damien told him Harley was okay. But Ray knew what Nathan meant.

"Yeah," he answered with a hoarse voice. Straightening up, Ray used the wet end of the towel to scrub the dried blood from his face. He was rough with the towel, leaving his skin reddened. Water ran down his throat, dropping from his chin, saturating his chest hair. Using the dry end of the towel, Ray blotted himself dry.

"Better?" Nathan asked.

"Better," he answered on a sigh. Ray pulled his clean shirt from his ruck, pulling it on over his head. The blood on his pants was dried to black and he needed to get them off. Quickly, Ray shoved them down his legs and onto the floor. His skivvy shorts were saturated with blood, and the tops of his thighs were coated in it. He stripped off his shorts, too.

Ray rinsed the blood out of the towel, careful not to wring it too dry. He scrubbed hard at all the blood he could see, turning his skin an angry red. Rinsing the towel, the entire thing ended up soaking wet. Ray struggled to get all the blood out of the hair on his legs, dripping water onto the floor so that it puddled at his feet.

"Looks like you got it all, man. Good job." Nathan's voice sounded cheerful.

Ray startled. He'd forgotten Nathan was there. Glancing up, he found Nate leaning a shoulder against the door, looking like he was reading his cell phone. Taking in Nathan's casual demeanor, Ray started to relax.

"Yeah, you're right." Ray dumped the towel into the bowl of the sink. Grabbing a dry one from the stack, he dried himself off. Tossing the towel onto the floor, Ray cleaned up the puddle of water beneath his feet.

His hands were still stiff and uncooperative, but Ray finally managed to get himself dressed. He almost asked Nathan for help tying his shoelaces, but he managed to get it done on his own. Stuffing his ruined uniform into his ruck, Ray looked up to find Nathan had wrung out the wet towel and folded everything back into a neat stack.

"You have to feel better now," Nathan said as he collected the towels and Ray's rucksack. "It won't make waiting easier, but it will make it a little less miserable."

Ray did feel better, physically anyway. He was relieved that his uniform pants didn't scrape and scratch against his skin anymore. "Hey, thanks, man," he said awkwardly, his voice rough. "I appreciate this."

"Of course, buddy. I wouldn't be anywhere else." Nathan tone was as serious as his expression. Ray hated being smothered with pity. He hated inconveniencing his friends by asking anyone for help. It was different with Nathan, though. Ray didn't feel overwhelmed, and he knew Nate didn't judge him.

When they exited the restroom Ray's stomach plummeted as he realized the crowd had grown a lot. His throat tightened as so many people recited hollow platitudes. They meant well, but Ray didn't have the strength to keep up small talk with a group this size.

As if he was reading Ray's thoughts, Nathan began to run interference. He was polite and friendly, but he still managed to keep people off Ray and to keep the chatter to a minimum. Collapsing into a chair, Ray sighed heavily.

A Styrofoam container and a fresh bottle of water appeared on the small table beside him. "You need to eat something," Nathan said in a low voice. "When Damien's job is finished, yours begins. You need your strength so you can nurse Harley back to health."

Ray knew Nathan was right, but his stomach argued. Setting the container on his lap, Ray slowly worked his way through the food. It was all tasteless, but with each bite it got a little easier. As he ate, Ray tuned out the conversation around him. He didn't have the energy for small talk. Quiet laughter abruptly captured his attention, jarring him out of his own thoughts. Ray closed the food container and set it aside.

Nathan briefly laid a comforting hand on Ray's knee, but he kept his attention on the deputy who was speaking. Ray heard his and Harley's names, and he glanced up in surprise. Everyone in the room sat listening to Rick Weldon as he told the story of a radio call Ray and Harley had assisted on. Ray remembered the incident, but he'd never heard the events from Rick's point of view.

"Ray was trailing right behind Harley, and I was following him as cover. Harley had his head down, following the track along the side of the road. The dirt shoulder dropped off to an embankment that was covered in these really tall reeds, overgrown from the tributary that runs beneath the road." Several deputies nodded, familiar with the location. "Harley veers off the road and down the embankment. Ray keeps following, shoving through the reeds like they're nothing. I was sure Harley'd lost the scent and was just wandering around exploring, but I kept following." Several people in the room chuckled, obviously relating to Rick's unfounded moment of doubt. "We come out of the reeds into a clearing where we know there's a homeless camp. Harley's head is still down, he's totally focused, and he starts walking right through the encampment. There are people everywhere, there's food, and there's garbage strewn all over the place. Those without a tent have their bedrolls laid out, right in the open. Ray's telling everybody just to stand still, the dog's perfectly safe, we'll be out of their way in just a minute. Harley starts weaving through the encampment. I'm *positive* he's going to lose the scent this time, or get distracted by the food, the trash, or all the different people smells."

"You should have known better than to doubt Harley," someone said from the far side of the room. There was humor and affection in his voice.

"Cut me some slack," Rick replied. "It was the first time I'd covered Ray and Harley." Ray thought back and realized that Rick had transferred from another patrol station, just a few weeks before this incident. "So, Harley is marching through this camp, stepping through things, and over things. He walks over about half a dozen bedrolls, gives each one a sniff, but never stops moving forward. Ray and I got hung up inside the camp, stepping over garbage, trying *not* to step on the bedrolls, and colliding with the camp residents. When we finally get clear, we see Harley disappearing down the far side of a slope leading to the edge of a pond. Finally, Harley lifts his head and comes to a dead stop. Ray and I catch up, and Harley's just standing there, staring hard at a cluster of reeds on the bank of the pond. We're looking around, trying to figure out what the deal was, but there's nothing. Harley finally sits down, but he just keeps staring at that same bunch of reeds."

"Let me guess, Ray said, 'Well, that's not exactly an alert, but...' and then says something that makes it seem like he can read Harley's mind," Ryan—the handler from Fallbrook—said quietly, grinning at Rick.

"Exactly," Rick replied exuberantly. "Ray goes, 'Well, that's not exactly an alert, but it *is* a change in behavior', and he breaks leather on his holster."

"It's fucking supernatural, how he knows what Harley's trying to communicate. I wish I knew how they do it." Ryan actually sounded awestruck.

"I figured Ray's hand on the butt of his gun was *my* signal to position myself as cover," Rick said, raising his arms to demonstrate. "But I had no idea what the hell was going on, or what to expect. Then Ray goes, 'We know you're hiding in the bushes. Just come out now, with your hands where we can see them, and I won't have to send the dog in after you', and he sounds like he's bored with this whole thing."

"Did the suspect come out?" asked Jennings.

"His head suddenly pops up above the reeds, hands raised, and starts begging Ray not to let the dog bite him," replied Rick, shaking his head slowly, and looking amazed. "So, Ray tells him to come out quickly, follow orders, and behave himself. He told him not to resist, and don't give us a hard time, and Harley wouldn't have a reason to bite him."

Quiet laughter and other sounds of amusement rippled through the room, filling Ray with a warm feeling. He had no special memories of that incident;

it was just another successful track for Harley. The respect and admiration he glimpsed around the room surprised him, but it also filled him with pride.

"One more suspect in custody, no resistance," Ryan said with a chuckle. "'Cause nobody wants to tangle with Harley."

"Does anybody remember that one time, during the street fair, when the beer garden got too rowdy and we had to shut it down?" Deputy Tran asked, looking around at his fellow Vista deputies.

"Classic," someone murmured.

Tran seemed to take the lack of response as his cue to continue. "The beer garden was too wild for safety. There was too much noise, we'd had to break up several scuffles, and women were complaining about getting groped. The people running the garden decided to shut it down voluntarily, before somebody got hurt. The crowd ignored them when they announced the beer garden was closed and it was time to leave."

"And we all know how folks who have imbibed a lot *hate* it when their party ends," Nathan said dryly.

"A bunch of us went in and announced the beer garden was closed, everybody had to leave." Tran glanced around at his audience, smiling. "It was like we weren't even there. When we started to *insist* and *urge* a few partygoers toward the exit, things escalated. We were looking at physically having to restrain people, make some arrests, and none of us wanted all the hassles. Somebody got on the radio with Sergeant Lerner to advise him of what was about to go down, and he said to standby while he gave it one final try."

Ray knew how this story ended, and he didn't remember anything special happening. He thought about it from the perspective of the other deputies who'd worked with him. Maybe it was a little funny.

Tran was enthusiastic about the story. He gesticulated sharply for emphasis. "We all took up positions around the group, ready to contain them if necessary. They were still ignoring us though. Then the sergeant steps into the entrance. He was wearing those dark, wrap-around shades, and he held on to that short little leash, while Harley strained against his harness. It looked like Sarge was struggling to keep this *gigantic* vicious dog from attacking everyone. It got a little quieter, but the horde still wasn't leaving. So, he walks to the back of the beer garden, Harley dancing around and pushing his huge chest against his harness. By the time he gets to the back wall, everybody's finally quiet.

The whole crowd was watching Sarge and Harley, not saying a word. Sergeant Lerner just stands there for several seconds, Harley sitting quiet beside him. All he does is give that command that tells Harley to bark like he's rabid. Harley stands up on all fours and unleashes that snarling bark of his on the crowd. That was all it took." Tran's expression grew smug. "Nobody in that mob said a word. They just all stood up and headed for the exit. That beer garden was *empty* just like *that*." Tran snapped the fingers of one hand.

The room filled with warm laughter. Ray couldn't help joining in. He admitted to himself that he could be dramatic when he wanted to, and the crowd's reaction to Harley was probably hilarious to everyone who knew it was all a bluff.

"Nobody got hurt, and nobody ended up spending the night in Central Booking," Tran declared. He sat back, his expression pleased.

"Yeah, we're all damn lucky Harley's on our team and we get to work with him," Nathan said solemnly. There were sounds of assent from all around the waiting room. Ray's throat tightened painfully with the realization that his fellow deputies not only trusted and respected Harley, they enjoyed working with him, too.

The door behind the reception desk opened, grabbing Ray's attention. Tony emerged from the depths of the hospital and glanced around the waiting room. His eyes widened in surprise. "Whoa. You multiplied," he said, as if to himself.

Ray leapt to his feet, quickly crossing to the counter. "How is Harley?" he demanded, more harshly than he'd intended.

"They're almost done, but Doctor D told me to come let you know," answered Tony. "Harley made it through the surgery just fine. The doc just has to finish stitching and bandaging him up, and then he says he'll come out and talk to you. He'll tell you what he found during surgery, and what's going to happen next."

Ray's legs went weak with relief. He blew out a tense breath, leaning heavily on the counter. Nathan was suddenly beside him, arm around Ray's shoulders and squeezing hard. Part of Ray wanted to punch the air and shout in triumph, another part wanted to find a dark, quiet corner so he could cry with happiness. "Thank you, Tony," Ray said gratefully, shaking the kid's hand. "I appreciate you letting me know."

"No problem," said Tony, glancing around the crowded room. "How's everybody doing? Is there anything I can get for anybody?"

"You've been a lot of help," Nathan said quietly. "Thank you."

Tony gathered up the used and unused towels before he disappeared back into the hospital. Ray was suddenly surrounded by friends and fellow K9 handlers. He shook hands, tolerated a few back-slapping hugs, as he thanked everyone for showing their support. He also thanked them for sharing their stories about Harley, so he could see how helpful his dog was.

Ryan stepped up and gave Ray a brief hug. "Hey man, this is great news. I'm so damn happy Harley is okay. We'll stick around to see what the doc has to say, then we'll all get out of your hair."

"Thank you for being here, bud," Ray said. He managed a small smile as his eyes filled.

The inner door opened again and this time, Damien appeared. He looked haggard, but something in his expression told Ray things were okay. He met Damien as he came around the back of the reception desk, needing to hear the words that Harley would be fine.

Damien grasped Ray's bicep with a firm grip that was calming and reassuring. His skin was shiny and slick, his scrubs were darkened where he'd sweat through them. His eyes held compassion, despite the dark shadows of fatigue beneath them. His full mouth curved upward slightly, and the sick feeling in Ray's gut lessened.

"What's the good news, Doc?" Nathan asked from just behind Ray's shoulder.

"Harley came through surgery as well as I could have hoped," Damien replied. "Luisa and Tony are setting him up with a comfortable bed, getting his IVs going. I had him under general anesthesia, and he's on some really excellent pain medication, so he's going to sleep for a long while yet."

"How bad was it?" Ray could finally ask the question, now that he knew Harley was okay.

"The first thing I had to do was control the bleeding," Damien replied. "It took me awhile to suture the blood vessels back together, because they're small, but I got it done. Then I had to see if the knife had penetrated deep enough to damage any internal organs. I had to be very, very careful, because a small nick to an intestine from the tip of the knife could be fatal, if I didn't catch it and repair it."

"It sounds like you found something," Ray said, dread sinking into his belly again.

"I checked every inch of intestine for leaks, and I located one that was easy to repair," answered Damien. "There was no damage to any other organs. I closed him up, and Luisa and Tony put a bright, pretty bandage around him."

Relief flooded Ray's entire body. "Thank you," he said, taking a deep breath and blowing it out slowly. "How long before he wakes up? Can I see him?"

"He's going to sleep most of the night." Damien said, looking around at the assembled deputies. "We're going to keep a close eye on him." He met Ray's eyes again. "We've got room for you to sit with him. Beyond that, there isn't anything more anyone can do for him. One of us can even help get you home in the morning."

"Can I see him right now?" Ray asked anxiously. He believed Damien's words, but it wouldn't feel real until he saw Harley with his own eyes.

"Sure. I'll take you back. Do you have any personal gear you need to grab?" Damien glanced around the room.

Nathan handed Ray his rucksack. "Your gun belt is in the trunk of your patrol car. Your car key is in your bag, along with your cell phone and wallet. Call me if you need help getting home. Call me if you need *anything*."

"Thank you, man." Ray awkwardly pulled Nathan in for a hug. "Thanks for everything." He didn't have the words that would tell Nate just how much his help meant to Ray.

When Nathan pulled away and moved to shake Damien's hand, Ryan appeared directly in front of Ray. "That's fucking awesome, bro. I'm so glad Harley's okay."

Ray sought out Tran and Jennings, shaking each of their hands vigorously. "I owe both of you so damn much. I won't ever be able to pay you back for all your help tonight."

"Nah, man," Jennings said, waving off Ray's words. Tran echoed Jennings' words with a negative shake of his head. "Harley's one of us. We take care of each of other."

"You'd do the same for any of us," Tran said firmly.

Nathan began herding all the deputies out the front door. It was late, but Ray felt a little better knowing they'd all still be able to get a decent amount of sleep before their shift started that afternoon.

Damien made sure the outside door was secure again. He held the inside door open for Ray as he shut off the waiting room lights. Ray paused just inside the hospital, looking around anxiously for Harley.

"Here. Put your gear in my office." Damien didn't give Ray a chance to argue. He took the ruck from Ray's shoulder, setting it just inside the door of a darkened office. "He's right over here." Damien extended one hand, showing Ray which direction he needed to go. He pressed his other hand to the small of Ray's back, encouraging him to move forward.

Ray let Damien guide him to the far corner of the huge room. Damien's hand at his back was comforting, his warmth spreading through Ray, strengthening him. Seeing the IV poles supporting several full bags of fluid, he resisted the urge to cross the distance at a run. Damien led Ray past the treatment table they'd all gathered around earlier, finally giving him his first glimpse of Harley's unconscious form.

Chapter 10: Secrets Shared In The Deep Of The Night

Ray stumbled slightly, leaning into Damien's hand against his back. He swallowed a sob, sounding strangled. Harley was so still and fragile looking. He was nestled in a large pile of blankets on the floor, his entire middle encircled by a bright purple adhesive bandage. The rise and fall of his chest was the only sign that Harley was alive. All Ray could think of was putting his hands over Harley's ribcage and feeling the beat of his heart.

"He's asleep," Damien said softly, leaning in. "I'm keeping him sedated so he doesn't get antsy. It makes it easier to keep his IVs in, and his bandage in place. Sleep is also the best thing for him right now."

"He really is going to be okay." Ray hoped saying the words aloud—hearing them in his own voice—would make it finally feel real.

Damien stepped behind him, placing both hands on Ray's shoulders, and giving them an encouraging squeeze. "His prognosis is excellent," he said, just above a whisper. "You did everything you could for Harley, and you did it all right. You got him to me quickly, which made a lot of difference."

He didn't trust himself to speak, so Ray nodded, letting Damien know he'd heard him. He remembered his own desperate, single-minded need to get Harley to Damien, knowing Damien would keep him alive. That memory helped Ray to find his voice. "Thank you for saving him," he said, sounding as raw and as drained as he felt.

Damien's body was warm and reassuring, pressed against Ray's back. He was intensely aware of Damien's warm breath drifting across his ear. A shiver ran through him, which Damien seemed to misunderstand, rubbing both palms up and down Ray's arms.

Luisa appeared in the open doorway directly across from them. She gave Ray an encouraging smile. "Harley's a strong and healthy boy," she said, kneeling down on the thick stack of blankets. "Doctor D didn't have any trouble getting him all fixed up." Luisa checked Harley's mouth, making sure his tongue didn't block his breathing. She checked the IV needle in his foreleg, held securely with the same purple bandage encircling his middle. When she was satisfied the bags were dripping at the appropriate rate, Luisa used her stethoscope to listen along the length of Harley's body. When she finished, she gave Ray another smile as she rose to her feet. "Show him all the love you can, just be careful of his IV lines."

Luisa gave his arm a pat as she stepped passed Ray. His brain was sluggish with exhaustion from worry, stress, and relief, making him vulnerable to Damien's offered comfort. Belatedly, Ray realized they stood too closely, touched too easily, for a strictly professional relationship. Luisa had to have seen it but hadn't said a word. Her kindness and compassion felt limitless; a balm to his ragged nerves. Luisa was gone before Ray realized he needed to thank her for taking such good care of Harley, even before tonight.

Tony materialized next, placing two bottles of water on the floor against the wall. He paused to stroke Harley's head a few times before he disappeared through the door Luisa had entered from.

"Thanks, Tony," Damien called after him.

When Damien gave his shoulders a firm push, Ray finally managed to move. In a few steps, he was beside Harley's makeshift bed. Carefully, Ray knelt on the generous stack of blankets, the outside of one knee against Harley's spine. Sitting back on his heels he whispered, "Hey, buddy. How you doin'?" Ray gently pressed both open palms to Harley's deep chest, searching for the feel of his beating heart beneath his ribs. "How's my boy? It looks like they're taking really good care of you." Harley's heartbeat was strong and steady beneath Ray's hands. "That's my good boy. You gotta rest up so you can get better and come back to work, okay buddy?" He ran his hands over Harley's head and along the length of his body.

It was bizarre, Harley not responding when he was given praise and affection. He looked peaceful, at least. Ray could almost pretend he was only sleeping. He shifted to rest on one hip, burying his fingers in Harley's thick fur.

Tony and Damien were both suddenly there, each carrying a large stack of pillows and blankets. They set them down against the wall close to Harley's bedding.

"Thank you, Tony," Damien said quietly. "Now get out of here." He smiled to ease the sting of his words.

"You sure neither of you need anything else?" Tony asked, glancing between Damien and Ray.

Ray shook his head, surprised to be included in Tony's inquiry. "Thank you for all your help," he said, meaning it.

"I'm glad we could help Harley," Tony said with surprising solemnity. "You had everybody scared, Sergeant. But Harley took good care of you, so we'll take real good care of him." He headed for the rear exit. "Good night, Doc."

"Good night, Tony." Damien looked pale. Giving Ray a wan smile, he knelt down and arranged several blankets until they resembled a bedroll. He leaned several pillows against the wall.

Ray was suddenly awash in a fresh flood of guilt. He'd scared everyone who cared about Harley, by letting him get hurt. Ray's thoughts were sluggish, it was like he could actually feel his brain struggling to make sense of some things. Damien still wore a tense expression. Ray gave himself a mental ass kicking for not realizing sooner what kind of an emotional toll all this probably had on Damien.

"Okay, everything's cleaned up and locked down," Luisa said, appearing silently from somewhere. "Doctor D, are you *sure* you don't want me to stay? I was already on the calendar for the night, anyway. It's been a rough night for you." She smiled indulgently at Ray.

A look of dread crossed Damien's face. The expression cleared just as quickly as it had appeared, but Ray knew he'd seen it. "Everything's okay now," Damien replied evenly. "I don't expect any complications, but I want to stay and monitor Harley. There's absolutely no need for two of us to be here all night."

"As long as you're sure." Luisa's tone made it clear *she* wasn't sure. "Tony made sure everyone in the kennels is fed, watered, and medicated. Becky knows to call your cell phone if she has to escalate a triage."

"Thank you, Luisa." With a tired smile, Damien hooked his thumb toward the door. "Now go. And hit the lights on your way out."

Slinging a large, colorful bag over her shoulder, Luisa turned to leave. "I'm glad we were able to help Harley," she called over her shoulder. "That was your one free pass, though. You don't get to scare us like that again, Ray. Good night. You boys behave."

Luisa flipped some switches as she left, shutting off all the overhead florescent bulbs. Emergency lighting in the ceiling cast everything in shadows. Ray gave a relaxed sigh, the diffused light and absence of florescent hum was a relief.

A comfortable quiet settled around them; the dimmed lighting cast the room in pleasant shadows. Ambient sounds swirled gently, carried on the air from medical machines scattered around the room. Mechanical hums and clicks mingled with the soft animal sounds drifting in from sleeping and drowsy patients. There was something soothing about a puppy snoring quietly, while a gray-muzzled Labrador gave a contented sigh. Ray's angry, inflamed nerves were mollified by the muted illumination.

Christ, he'd been a self-centered dick all night. He'd let Harley get hurt, and then treated everyone like he was the only one who'd been scared and worried. When he remembered Luisa's parting words, it occurred to Ray that Damien's staff was all aware the two of them had a personal relationship. As long as Damien got the respect, the loyalty, he deserved, Ray was fine with it.

All of a sudden, it felt like someone threw a power switch inside of Ray. Unable to hold himself upright any longer, he slid down onto his side, cradling his head on one arm. As gently as he could, Ray draped his second arm over Harley's shoulder. It had been a hell of a night, and now his head spun, despite his physical exhaustion.

Ray was surprised when Damien dropped down onto the bedroll he'd fashioned, Harley's head within inches of his right leg. Beside his left hip, Damien unrolled a towel that held a few things—tools maybe?—that Ray didn't recognize. He added his tablet and his cell phone, so Ray figured Damien was settling in with everything he needed to monitor Harley's condition throughout the night.

As if he'd heard Ray's thoughts, Damien leaned forward to more firmly secure the blanket around Harley. "You know him best," Damien said softly, "if you think he's getting cold, go ahead and carefully tuck another blanket around him."

"Got it," Ray whispered. With Harley pressed against him, Ray felt his warmth. He watched Harley's chest rise and fall as he breathed, his own arm matching the rhythmic motion. Ray had awakened from the nightmare of Harley getting injured to the welcome reality that he was alive and on the mend.

Damien was so close, but it was like they were in separate rooms. Ray wanted to feel Damien against him—all around him. He wanted to close his eyes, nuzzle his nose to the warm, silky skin behind Damien's ear, and inhale.

Damien's scent lingered there, laced with a hint of his cologne, and mingled with fresh, salty sweat. If Ray moved his hand mere inches, he could grasp Damien's leg. He could ask silently, for the rapture and solace he always found in Damien's body.

Or he could choose not to be an asshole. Damien had been the one to save Harley, after Ray had put him in harm's way. He could start with a *mea culpa*, undoubtedly he should make a display of his gratitude, and apologize for putting them all through this hellish night.

After all the hours he and Damien had spent together, in these past weeks, Ray should know the right things to say, and to do for Damien. He'd thought they'd reached the point where he and Damien fell easily into one another's bodies.

Ray opened his mouth to say comforting words to Damien, but that's not what came tumbling out. "I figured you guys would have a couple cots back here," he blurted. Ray was lost; completely adrift.

"We do," Damien replied. He shifted against the stacked pillows, quietly working on his tablet with a stylus. "They're in another room, though. Kinda hard to monitor my patient from a distance." He grabbed a pillow from the second pile of bedding and set it beside Ray's head. "You should get comfortable, so you don't end up with a crick tomorrow."

"Thanks." Ray cradled the pillow beneath his head. "And thank you again, for everything you've done tonight." Those words were still embarrassingly inadequate, and they probably always would be, but he was at a loss for anything else to say. "I'm just sorry you're hanging out here, all night."

Damien studied Ray for several interminable moments, his blue eyes inscrutable behind his dark-rimmed glasses. "You're welcome. I'm glad I was able to help."

"I knew you would," Ray blurted, surprising himself. He held Damien's gaze as he buried his fingers in the thick fur of Harley's shoulder. "I knew he'd be okay once I got him to you."

"I appreciate your faith in me," Damien said. "Especially since it was the luck of the draw that I was on duty tonight."

Ray drew his brows together in surprise and confusion. "I didn't race him to the *hospital*," he said quickly, needing Damien to understand. "It wasn't this *place* I knew I needed to get him to. It was *you* I needed to get him to."

Damien's expression showed doubt. He gave Ray a hesitant half-smile, as if he was waiting for a punchline. "Even though Doctor Reese is a more experienced surgeon?"

Ray watched his own fingers comb through Harley's dark coat as he weighed his words. "I know you're a good veterinarian. But I also know you like Harley. I knew you'd fight like hell to keep him alive." He looked back up at Damien to see if he understood. Right now, Ray didn't trust himself not to get weepy.

Damien pressed his lips into a thin line. Ray saw the tightening of muscles that meant Damien held his jaw clenched. His eyes looked wet, but his only answer was a quick nod of his head. They were both silent for several moments. Ray closed his eyes, listening to the reassuring sound of Harley breathing. He was so damn grateful he was still able to do that.

With Harley's warmth, and the steady sound of his breathing, Ray started to believe that everything was finally okay. He dredged up the courage to ask the scariest question of all. "How close of a call was it?"

"It had the potential to be a worst-case scenario, but it didn't go that way," Damien replied, twisting the stylus between his fingers. "His wound is serious, but you guys slowed down his rate of blood loss. You were fast and efficient about getting him help." He took a deep breath, letting it out slowly, watching his own hands as he fidgeted. "Worrying about something that didn't go wrong will only rob you of the energy you'll need to help Harley get better." Damien looked as though he wanted to say more but thought better of it.

Ray thought about Iraq, and how things had gone down back then. His fellow Marines had limited resources in the field and were still taking fire as they got the casualties loaded onto the helo. Memories were so fucking exhausting.

He jolted awake with a gasp. Ray didn't even remember closing his eyes. Someone moved nearby. Ray pushed up, bracing himself on an elbow. His vision cleared to reveal Damien leaning over Harley, removing his stethoscope from his ears. Ray's heart leapt in his chest, his throat tightening so he couldn't speak.

"Just checking on my patient," Damien whispered, giving Ray a reassuring smile. "Everything's still just fine." He examined the IV lines before returning to his place against the wall.

"How long was I asleep?" Ray asked, sitting up. He rubbed his fingers hard over his eyelids, trying to banish the remnants of panic.

"About an hour," replied Damien. "I'm sure you feel a little better."

Ray did an internal status check. "A little." He felt like he was getting in control of his emotions, too. Knowing Harley's condition was stable helped, too.

"This second pile of blankets is for you," Damien announced, gesturing toward the folded fabric beside himself. "Stretch out, get comfortable, if you need to. You're fine where you are, though."

Ray was torn. The thought of stretching out fully on the bedroll was alluring. The thought of being wrapped up in Damien's arms was equally alluring. He scrubbed at his face, reminding himself that Harley's need for Damien's attention was greater. Looking down at Harley's peacefully slumbering form, Ray reached a hand out to rub his ear.

"There's water for you over here, too," Damien said on a sigh. Lifting his glasses from the bridge of his nose, he rubbed his eyes with a thumb and forefinger. He looked even more exhausted than he had earlier.

The urge to take Damien into his arms and soothe his exhaustion was powerful. He longed to take comfort from Damien's touch, while sharing his own strength. He didn't dare flout Damien's professionalism by defiling the place where he did his work.

Ray's mouth was dry from sleep. Getting to his knees, he spread the blankets, stacking the pillows against the wall. With a heavy sigh, he collapsed onto the bedroll, leaning his back against the stack of pillows. Reaching for the fresh bottle of water on the floor between them, Ray was acutely aware of Damien's immediacy.

He swallowed several mouthfuls of water. "Thank you," Ray said, setting the bottle aside. "I sure have said that to you a lot, tonight." He skimmed his hand over Harley's head, where it rested beside his left knee. "I don't think I'll ever say it enough."

"It's nice to know I'm appreciated," Damien said with a grin. Reaching forward, he scratched at Harley's chest. "You know I really like Harley. He has a great personality. And the two of you are too important, as a team, to lose."

Ray grasped desperately at the hope he felt at hearing Damien's words. "So...he'll be able to return to full duty?"

"I expect him to." Damien's reply was almost more than Ray could hope for. "As long as the incision heals properly—and I expect it to—he should be good as new."

"The fact he's even alive is the most important thing." Ray needed to be sure Damien didn't think his love for Harley was conditional. "But it would be sad to lose him as a partner while he's still in his prime."

He watched his own fingers curling into the fur at the back of Harley's neck. Damien's fingers brushed against Ray's as they both combed them through the same patch of Harley's fur. A familiar warm tingle spread through Ray's hand. He lightly skated his finger along the side of Damien's, prolonging the touch, silently encouraging more. Ray enjoyed the feel of Damien's touch; he enjoyed the way he felt in Damien's presence. Ray liked who he was when he was around Damien. He wished he could think of a reason Damien might feel the same way about him.

They sat quietly for several comfortable moments, only their fingers touching. Damien chuckled softly, sounding playful, as he hooked his finger over Ray's and trapped it. "Harley and I have become very good friends in the last several weeks, I hope he doesn't hold a grudge for tonight."

Ray swallowed back his laugh so it ended up somewhere between a choke and a snort. "With the way you bribe him with treats, he'll forgive you for anything." He always liked it when Damien mentioned a future that included both of them. "I think he's been missing you the last few days. You're overdue in bringing him his snacks." Ray gave a short, self-conscious laugh. Their work schedules in the last week had made it impossible for them to see each other for the past five days. Ray had been missing Damien. He'd been missing Damien a lot. "If he wanted to visit you, he could have just gone off his feed. This was going a little too far."

Damien blessed Ray with one of his brilliant, blinding smiles. Ray returned the smile with one of his own, like he always did. It wasn't like he could control it. Damien covered Ray's entire hand with his own. Together, they curled their twined fingers into Harley's thick fur. Ray swallowed hard against the lump that formed in his throat. He didn't have to explain his job, or his bond with Harley, and Damien even played along with his jokes. If he didn't figure out quickly, how to give as much as he took, he was going to lose the best thing in his life.

Damien's smile faded, until his expression became dark with worry. He started to speak but stopped himself short both times. It scared the hell out of Ray and, reflexively, he gripped Damien's hand harder. "How close did *you* come to getting hurt tonight?" Damien finally asked, the words tumbling out of him in a hoarse whisper. He tightened his fingers around Ray's, as well.

The question shocked the hell out of him. It wasn't just his words, but also the fear in Damien's voice. Looking up, Ray found Damien's expression tense, his eyes wide with dread. "Nowhere near," Ray whispered in reply, meeting Damien's gaze steadily. He didn't like that Damien had experienced this worry, this fear, because of him. "Harley did his job, just like he's supposed to. He ran straight into a dark house, after an armed suspect, just because I asked him to."

Their joined hands still rested on Harley's shoulder, so Ray felt the shiver that ran through Damien's body. He needed to reassure Damien, but Ray sucked at giving comfort. Damien dropped his eyes from Ray's as he said, in a shaky voice, "Obviously, I know that someone stabbed Harley with a knife, but I don't know *how* it happened." The request for information was implied.

Ray had been so focused on Harley, he hadn't considered that Damien might have worried about *him*. Remembering some of Damien's words and actions from earlier, Ray felt like an even bigger asshole than he already had.

Haltingly at first, Ray told the story about tracking Juan Ramos. He explained his responsibilities and his concerns over an armed, barricaded suspect. He told Damien how he felt, sending Harley into a darkened house after Ramos. Harley didn't hesitate though, so Ray—and his fellow deputies—went home safe. Damien listened silently as Ray recounted his shock, and his sickening fear, when he realized Ramos had stabbed Harley with a Ka-Bar. "You know the rest," Ray said, clearing his throat in agitation. "Jennings and I applied pressure to the wound while Tran drove like a bat out of hell."

Lifting their joined hands, Damien pressed them to his chest. "That made all the difference," he murmured, nodding several times as if something had slotted into place. He leaned in close, so Ray had to meet his gaze. "You have no idea what it did to me, seeing you absolutely covered in blood, wearing this dazed expression." Damien's voice was raw and Ray thought he heard a tremor. As Ray studied him, Damien's eyes filled and he blinked furiously.

"Oh shit," Ray spat, rubbing his eyes hard with the fingers of his free hand.

He remembered exactly what his uniform had looked like, when he'd arrived at the hospital. He could imagine his expression too, knowing how shocked and scared he'd been for Harley's sake. "I'm sorry," he murmured, "I'm so fucking sorry. I knew Nathan called ahead, so it never occurred to me you might think I was hurt, too." If a suspect tried to take Ray on, Harley would be right there to protect him. He brought their hands—surprised they were still joined—to his lips and pressed a kiss to Damien's. "You were probably surprised as hell and worried shitless." Ray clasped Damien's hand between both of his own as he pressed kisses to Damien's fingers. "And you had to focus all your attention on Harley. You must think I'm a total dick, making the entire night all about what *I* went through."

Frowning, Damien closed his eyes and removed his glasses. He sat for several interminable moments, his breathing shaky, and his grip tight on Ray's hand. It was difficult, but Ray kept his mouth shut. He'd explained and apologized, now he just had to wait for Damien to tell Ray what he needed.

Damien swallowed audibly. "Nathan told me you were fine. I didn't press him for details, because I didn't know what he knew. About us, I mean. Since you were bringing Harley in yourself, I just figured you were uninjured."

"I know how I looked when we got here," Ray said quietly. "I'm sure it was a shock. You probably thought Nathan had been wrong." He felt the urge to pull Damien into his arms and whisper words of assurance into his ear. Ray was afraid his touch would be unwelcome, so he waited for Damien to give him some hint, or some clue. "And I realize now that you were just as worried about Harley as any of us. I was an oblivious dickhead not bothering to explain or comfort."

Damien finally opened his eyes and he looked exhausted. "You were covered in blood, Ray. Everything Nathan had told me didn't matter, you looked like you were bleeding out. And Harley was on the table in front of me, and he *really* was in danger of bleeding out. More than anything, I wanted to touch you, to make sure you were all right. You were counting on me to keep Harley alive, and I was scared shitless that if I lost him, I'd lose you, too." There was obvious pain in Damien's blue eyes now.

Ray took Damien's glasses from his unresisting fingers, setting them on the blanket beside him. He grasped both of Damien's hands, pressing his open palms to Ray's chest. "I'm fine. None of that blood was mine." Clasping a hand to the back of Damien's neck, Ray gently tugged him forward. He pressed his lips to Damien's temple and whispered. "Harley's going to be just fine, all because of you." Something between them was different. Damien's reaction was a lot fucking stronger than Ray had expected. He didn't understand how Damien would lose him, along with Harley.

Damien cleared his throat. He fisted Ray's T-shirt with both hands. With a subtle motion, Damien leaned closer, turning his face toward Ray. "Yeah. I got it," he said in a rough voice. "It was an emotional night, but everyone's gonna be okay." Damien abruptly pulled away. Releasing Ray's shirt, he sat up straight and reached for his glasses. As Ray watched in confusion, Damien's glasses became a mask, and he threw up an invisible shield. Ray had no fucking clue what the fuck had just happened.

Damien smoothly got to his knees as he brought his stethoscope to his ears. He listened all along Harley's length and checked his bandages before tucking the blanket back around him. Sitting back against the wall again, he picked up his tablet.

"He's still doing okay, isn't he?" Ray asked hesitantly. Damien's silence had a strange feel to it, and Ray felt compelled to probe it.

"Just fine," Damien replied without looking away from his tablet. His voice was low and smooth, like it was meant to be comforting. It sounded practiced, and Ray wondered when he'd become someone who needed to be managed. "He's still going to sleep for a while. Now is probably a good time to get some rest."

"You're going to get some sleep too, right?" Ray asked. "It's been a rough night on all of us. You as much as anybody."

"Yeah. I'm fine," Damien answered tightly, setting aside his tablet. "I'll close my eyes for a little while."

Ray was quickly learning to hate the word *fine*.

Leaning his head against the wall, Ray closed his eyes. He took a deep breath, releasing it slowly and trying to send all of his stress with it. He listened to the ambient sounds that surrounded Damien and him, surprised to find the rhythm was comforting and relaxing. Ray smiled reflexively at the soothing sound of Damien's sigh.

Managing to hold off sleep for a few moments longer, Ray opened his eyes slightly. He reached over and took Damien's hand in his own. Cradling the back of Damien's hand against his own palm, Ray twined their fingers. Resting their joined hands on the firm muscle of Harley's shoulder, Ray closed his eyes, relaxed, and encouraged sleep to overtake him. He was pleased with himself for not waking Damien. Of course, Damien might be playing possum, which was okay with Ray, too.

Chapter 11: Everything Is Clearer In The Bright Light Of Day

The feel of Damien's fingers slipping from his dragged Ray out of sleep. Opening his eyes, he found Damien leaning over Harley, stethoscope pressed to his chest. A glance at his watch told Ray they'd slept for close to an hour and a half. He watched Damien check Harley's eyes and mouth, and then detach one of the fluid bags from the I.V.

"Is everything still okay?" Ray asked in a rough voice. He watched Damien closely for any signs of the earlier tension.

"He's stable," Damien replied, sitting back against the wall. "It's okay if you want to lay down with Harley again. There's no need for both of us to have stiff necks and backs. He's also going to start waking up in a few hours. Your voice and your scent will be reassuring to him during his initial confusion."

That made sense. Remembering how disoriented he'd been after the first surgery on his arm, Ray could relate. "What happens after he wakes up?" he asked, taking a long drink from one of the water bottles that had been set out with the bedrolls. Whatever reason Damien had for putting up walls between them, it seemed to be forgotten. The knot in Ray's gut loosened.

"We need to get him on his feet," Damien answered, taking a drink from the second water bottle that had been set out. "He'll be very slow moving for a few days, just so long as he keeps moving. We need to get him eating and drinking, and once he can eliminate waste, we'll know he's well enough to go home."

Ray ran his hand over the unbandaged fur he could reach. "How long should that take?"

"As long as I'm sure the wound is healing, and there's no sign of infection," Damien replied as he adjusted his own pillows again. "It should just be a matter of days."

That surprised the hell out of Ray. His mind raced over the logistics of caring for Harley at home, the way he needed and deserved. "That soon? But he was stabbed and had surgery. Shouldn't someone have an eye on him twenty-four hours a day? What happens if something goes wrong?"

Damien didn't respond immediately. He finished making notes in his tablet and set it aside. "Harley's wound wasn't as severe as it seemed. With the bleeding controlled and the wound closed, the biggest concern is the low risk of infection." As Damien watched Ray, his brows drew together. "He's going to sleep a lot. You'll need to feed him soft food, and administer some meds, but nothing you can't handle."

"I can take several days off, but I'll have to go back to work fairly soon," Ray said, watching Harley's steady breathing. "He needs to have someone watching him in case he gets sick, or starts to bleed again, or spikes a fever, or gets too playful before he's ready." As competent as he might be at the day-to-day care, Ray had to be honest the he was no good when it came to extreme situations.

Damien still watched him with a puzzled expression. "You have a hell of a lot of friends and family who would happily look in on him, if not sit with him for your entire shift." He shrugged, as if Ray should have already considered this. "You also know that Nathan, and your fellow dog handlers, will provide any help you need."

Ray shook his head several times. Damien was genuinely trying to help, but he didn't know about Iraq. "It'd be safer for Harley to still be in the hospital when something goes wrong." He covered his forearm tattoo with his hand.

Damien's expression smoothed, his lips parting, his eyes widening in surprise. He started to speak but stopped himself, pausing for several long moments. Ray tensed, ready for Damien's arguments. He'd make him understand, eventually. Taking a deep breath, Damien spoke carefully, his voice soft and low. "I know you feel guilty about Harley getting hurt but try not to be." His words surprised the hell out of Ray. "Obviously I see a lot of sick and injured pets. It's shocking...and disgusting...how many are cases of neglect, or of deliberate injury. You're not to blame for Harley's injury."

Ray started to argue with Damien that he didn't know all the details. He was stopped by the warm memory of their late-night conversation, in the quiet room, holding hands. "I didn't prevent it from happening in the first place." Frustration made it difficult to keep his voice low.

Without missing a beat, Damien reached across the space separating them. It sent a warm tendril of pleasure curling into Ray's belly when Damien grasped his hand. Twining their fingers felt comfortable, like it was the most natural thing to do. "You can't judge what happened last night based on hindsight. You caught the bad guy, and you were careful to keep him from hurting anyone.

Harley was injured while doing his job, and not because you screwed up."

"I'm not questioning my actions," Ray said quickly. He took a deep breath, releasing it audibly. "I'm questioning my judgment." Two K9s had been wounded on his watches, so Ray needed to do a serious self-evaluation.

Damien didn't meet Ray's eyes. Instead, he studied their joined hands. "Your job is dangerous, sometimes. Which is why I worry about you." He dropped his voice on the last sentence, so it was almost a whisper.

Ray sat frozen, staring hard at Damien. He wished he could see Damien's blue eyes, so he could understand what had changed and what was happening. Damien was wound up still, but it all seemed directed at Ray, instead of Harley. His concern felt tinged with anger, and *that* had to be meant for Ray.

Understanding struck him like a fist in his gut. Damien wasn't making general statements about the danger of being a cop; he was scared specifically for Ray's well-being.

"Shit," he whispered fiercely, bringing Damien's hand to his lips for a kiss. "I'm a complete asshole. I'm sorry." He'd placed his wounded partner in Damien's hands and demanded a miracle. Damien had repaired a wound in Harley's flank that could have easily been in Ray's gut, all while keeping his own fears and worries to himself. Instead of looking to Damien to comfort him, Ray should be offering it.

"I was thinking *self-involved*," Damien said quickly. He finally met Ray's eyes. "You're right to be completely rocked by what happened. But something has you locked inside your own head, so you're oblivious to how deeply other people have been affected." Damien's pain and disappointment were plain to see.

Ray's guilt nearly swallowed him up. He also knew, without Damien having to tell him, they were at a critical place. Ray's next move meant the difference between a life filled with Damien, or one dotted with office visits to Doctor D.

He didn't even have to think about it. That should surprise Ray—the fact it didn't was something he'd think about later. Right now, was the time for him to tell Damien about Saija. He'd understand how deep that wound cut, back then as well as now.

"I want to tell you about something that happened to me during my last deployment to Iraq," Ray said carefully. He didn't look away from Damien's direct gaze. Because it felt right, he held on to Damien's hand. Ray's mouth and throat had both gone dry, so he took several long draughts of water.

"Is this the story of how your arm was injured?" asked Damien.

Throat tightening, Ray blinked back sudden tears. Damien rested their joined hands on top of Harley's shoulder. Ray enjoyed the warmth and soft fur against his skin. "Yeah. That's part of what happened anyway." With a shaky sigh, Ray traced the tattoo on his forearm, feeling the uneven surface of the scar tissue beneath.

Damien watched Ray's fingers as he glided them along the bright colored ink. "Did you lose a dog too?" he asked in a whisper.

Ray nodded in reply, not trusting himself to speak. At some point, the accuracy of Damien's intuition had stopped being surprising. Clearing his throat, Ray shifted against the pillows self-consciously.

"I'm sorry to hear that." Damien lifted his free hand, lightly skimming his fingers over Ray's tattoo. "This is a tribute to that dog?"

Ray shifted again. He tried to clear his throat once more but it came out a cough. "Saija. It's the Finnish version of the Hebrew Sara, which means princess or lady." He couldn't help grinning. "It suited her. She expected everyone to worship her."

"She earned everyone's worship, I bet," Damien replied, humor in his voice. "Was she your MWD in the Marines?"

"Yeah," Ray said in a rough voice. "She had a hell of a nose and she was fearless. She saved a lot of lives with all the explosives she detected."

"Tell me about her," Damien said gently.

Ray took a deep, fortifying breath. "We were eight weeks from the end of our deployment. When we got home, Saija was going to be retired. My hitch had about six months left, and I wasn't reenlisting, so they were letting me adopt her."

Damien stayed silent; his grip on Ray's hand was firm and comforting. Ray was grateful that Damien wasn't pressuring him to tell the story. He wanted to tell the story, though. He wanted to tell *Damien* the story. "Insurgents figured out that the canines had significantly reduced the effectiveness of their IEDs by detecting them before they could detonate. They'd started targeting the dogs, even paying bounties on them."

"Yeah, I've read about that in some of the professional journals," said Damien, still tracing the features of Ray's tattoo. "I have some patients who are retired MWDs. A few were either shot or caught in an explosion, so they have lingering health issues."

"Saija wasn't so lucky," Ray said sadly, his vision blurred by tears again. "My patrol started taking small arms fire. The hostiles were dug in behind the mud brick wall of a village, several dozen yards away. We returned fire as we took cover. I saw the grenade land and roll right toward Saija. There wasn't enough time to get her clear of the blast."

"Were you wounded in the same blast?" Now Damien skimmed his fingers over the rough, uneven edges of the scar on Ray's forearm, hidden by the elaborate tattoo of Saija's image.

"I wrapped my arm around her body and tried to drag her clear." Ray cradled Damien's hand between both of his now. "The blast broke my arm and shredded the muscle. They medevaced us both on the same helo, but Saija never regained consciousness. I spent the rest of my hitch in the Warrior Clinic in Bethesda, having my arm reconstructed."

"I'm sorry you had to go through all of that." Damien joined his free hand to their already clasped ones. "You must have thought history was repeating itself last night."

"Yeah. The fear, the dread, the *helplessness* were all the same." Ray avoided Damien's gaze, instead watching their joined hands. Ray knew he didn't have to explain or justify his bond with Saija. "When Saija was wounded, it seemed like it took hours for the helicopter to arrive, then it felt like the flight to the hospital lasted for hours. It was only minutes, though. And they were already working to save Saija."

"And your own injury meant you couldn't help. You couldn't even comfort her."

Ray gave a weary nod. Sniffling again, he closed his eyes, picturing Saija's lifeless body as he'd seen her lying in the hospital. Losing her had hurt every bit as much as losing a fellow Marine. He'd been so afraid he was going to have to relive that pain with Harley. "I was able to help with Harley's bleeding last night. I got to reassure and comfort him. But driving from the scene to the hospital seemed to take years, even though I knew it was only a few minutes."

"I'm so glad the outcome was different this time," Damien said fiercely. Ray was taken aback by his ferocity. "No vet likes to lose a patient, but Harley has a special place in my heart. Seeing you covered in his blood was shocking; I thought I'd come close to fucking losing you. And I was so fucking scared that if I couldn't save Harley, you'd hold it against me."

Ray had never seen Damien so earnest—so *intense*. It seemed like Damien's still waters ran deeper than Ray had first thought. It surprised him that this had Damien worried, because Ray had never even thought of it. That Damien had, meant Ray had a lot of making up to do. "I was never in that much danger, and you deserved to know that, right way. You also need to know that I'd never hold something like this against you." Ray spoke solemnly, giving his words weight and meaning. "I know you do everything you can for your patients. I know you feel a special affection for the working dogs, too. You understand the depth and strength of my bond with Harley, so I don't have to explain or justify it. And your staff reflects that, too. I'm grateful for the kindness and compassion you all showed us. The medical staff that treated Saija and me should take lessons from you."

Damien's expression became pained. "I can guess; she was just a dog, the Marines will give you another one, the important thing was that *you* survived."

Ray's laugh was mirthless. "The vet and the animal health techs understood, but they weren't the ones in charge of *my* care." He struggled to swallow past the lump that formed in his throat.

Scowling darkly, Damien asked, "Were you able to say good-bye, at least?"

"Barely," Ray answered. "Only after my command insisted. It was *too disruptive to the routine of my caregivers* they told me. I'm grateful to all of you for not belittling my feelings, and for trying to make the long wait bearable." He paused, considering his words. This wasn't about apologizing for being a dick, it was about taking a huge risk. "I'm not good at this; at talking about how I feel and apologizing."

Damien looked at him with wide eyes. "You've been doing a pretty good job."

"I have to," Ray said quickly. "It's important. *You're* important." Damien started to speak, but he stopped by abruptly closing his mouth. He looked as nervous as Ray felt, like his heart raced and his stomach quivered. "I know how I made you feel, bursting in here with Harley's blood all over me. I've had to leave wounded friends in the hands of the corpsman and complete my mission."

"You didn't get hurt though," Damien interjected. "Once I realized what was going on, I was fine. I focused on what I had to do for Harley."

"But I've been sitting here with you for several hours, and all I've talked about is Harley. How I felt when he got hurt, how scared I was, how worried I am, and how I let him down."

"It was traumatic for you, as much as it was for Harley..." Damien was so damn generous, but Ray didn't dare let himself be lulled by it this time.

"You had a hell of a night, too," Ray interrupted, sounding harsher than he'd meant to. "You need to talk about it. And there are some things *we* should talk about. Even if I hadn't had my head up my ass last night, I'd have kept everything distant and professional."

Damien's expression softened, looking almost sympathetic. "I expected that. My staff knows we've been on a couple of dates together, but they know to be discreet in front of other deputies."

"Thank you," Ray said, a familiar affection welling up in his chest. He gently grasped the back of Damien's neck, trying to ease the tension he felt beneath his fingers. "This is about more than a couple of dates, too." Even as he tugged Damien closer, Ray caught his look of surprise. Pressing a kiss to Damien's temple, he nuzzled at Damien's thick hair, enjoying the scent of him. "I don't go around waving rainbow flags—on or off duty—but it's also not a deep, dark secret." Ray felt Damien's quiet chuckle.

"I can't really picture you getting in people's faces with rainbow banners, anyway," Damien said through his laughter. "I didn't know how worried I was allowed to be for *you* last night. So, I hid all of what I was feeling," he said soberly. "What is it you think *we* should talk about?" Damien pulled back, leaning against the pillows again. His expression was hesitant, and also resigned.

"We've talked about how fucked up things got last night," Ray answered. "And how we felt about all the shit that went on. But why?"

"Why what?" Damien asked, looking apprehensive. "Why do we worry about each other? We're friends." He laughed wickedly. "And there's the fact we've fucked a few times."

Ray had to laugh at Damien's deliberate understatement. "More than a few times." Growing serious, he waited for Damien to meet his gaze again. "Is that all it is?" he asked quietly. "Are we just friends with some really hot fucking benefits?"

Damien became very still, his expression blank. "I don't know. You tell me."

Ray made a mental note never to play poker with Damien—unless it was strip poker.

Ray glanced around the dim room, finally letting his gaze settle on Harley's sleeping form. He ran his palms over his thighs nervously. He'd tried to get Damien to take the big risk, and had it tossed back at him. Ray could either be a total chicken shit, or he could tell Damien all the things he deserved to hear.

"No, that's not all we are." He turned to see how Damien was reacting to his words. "We're friends, but that's only part of it. I like all the time we spend together. Not just in bed, either—although that *is* pretty fucking awesome." Ray liked the way Damien's cheeks flushed as he smiled and glanced away. "I like the way certain things make me think about you, throughout my day. I like that we can talk about almost anything, but we're also comfortable sitting quietly. I want to be someone you can lean on. Someone you rely on." Ray fell silent, leaving the next step to Damien.

Drawing his knees up to his chest, Damien wrapped his arms around his legs. "Does all this mean you want to have an official relationship? That you want to see where we can take this?"

Ray shrugged. It wasn't exactly what he'd meant, but Damien was on the right track. "I think we've had a relationship for a little while now, we just haven't talked about it. And I want to do whatever we need to, to keep it going. How does that sound?"

Damien nodded wordlessly. He started with a small grin, growing into the wide, brilliant smile that always weakened Ray's knees and made his heart pound. "That sounds good. It sounds right." He tilted toward Ray slightly.

Leaning in, Ray met Damien halfway into the space between them. Resting their foreheads together, Ray whispered, "Come home with me in the morning? Once we know Harley's okay."

"Yes," Damien replied, placing a soft kiss on Ray's lips. "Yes, of course."

Ray felt better about the future than he had since before Harley was hurt. The world felt right, finally. He had faith that Harley was really going to be okay. Knowing Damien shared Ray's feelings, and they were both committed to making a future together made Ray's heart sing.

· · · ·

THE THUMP OF HARLEY'S tail against the blankets was the first sign he was waking up. The earliest of the hospital staff had arrived to check on the patients in the kennels. Damien asked for a small amount of water and wet food while he took Harley's temperature.

They rolled up the blankets and pillows so a vet tech could put them away. Ray sat talking to Harley, scratching at his neck. Damien detached the IV fluids but left the needle for the time being. He disappeared for several minutes, while Ray watched awareness return to Harley.

Ray needed to take a piss, but he wasn't going to leave Harley in anyone's care, except for Damien's. Only when he reappeared did Ray get directions to the head.

When he returned, he found Damien stroking Harley's head, murmuring to him quietly. Harley's eyes were heavy lidded and he licked at his muzzle repeatedly. He responded to Damien with an occasional flick of his tail.

When Ray knelt back down, Harley's eyes widened slightly, and his tail thumped more rhythmically. He moved his paws and lifted his head slightly.

"He's coming around," Damien said quietly. "He looks good so far."

Harley came around slowly. Most of the hospital staff stopped by to show him affection, even if they'd never worked with him in the clinic before. They all cared because he was a police K9, and he was injured. Ray appreciated that deeply.

When Harley was ready, Ray and Damien helped him up onto his stomach. He was obviously still groggy as he slowly looked around, weaving slightly despite having so much contact with the ground. Harley licked at Ray's hand distractedly, almost like he wasn't even aware of what he was doing.

When Harley was a little more awake, Ray finally urged him to drink some water from a bowl. When his eyes opened a little wider, and he was a little steadier, Harley showed interest in the wet dog food. He ate slowly, which seemed strange to Ray as he watched. He was so used to Harley bolting down his food with exuberance and enthusiasm.

It was midmorning when Ray was able to coax Harley up onto all four paws. He was still a little wobbly but managed to steady himself. He slowly followed Ray through the kennels and out a second exterior door. The small patch of fenced-in grass caught his interest for a few minutes as he walked the perimeter, sniffing at everything.

Ray followed in Harley's wake as Damien monitored his progress closely. Ray felt a wave of sympathy as he watched Harley struggle to find a way to relieve himself, despite his discomfort and limited mobility. Finally giving up on lifting his leg, Harley found success in a partial crouch. As they approached him, Damien grinned in spite of his obvious exhaustion.

"He's definitely on the mend," said Damien, holding the door open for Harley and Ray to reenter the hospital.

"You have no idea how relieved I am," Ray replied.

"I think I do," Damien said, running his palm firmly up and down Ray's back. It was comforting and affectionate, a combination Ray suspected only Damien could make him feel with a simple touch.

Harley was more than happy to crawl into a large, floor-level kennel. He was protected from the cold, hard metal floor by a thick nest of towels and blankets. He laid down carefully on his side, drifting off to sleep almost immediately. The hospital staff had Damien's instructions and orders for the day. They would monitor Harley throughout the day, providing pain meds if he seemed uncomfortable. Seeing the small army of caring people, all dedicated to looking after Harley, bled away the last of Ray's tension. He was left feeling weak and exhausted.

Damien gently steered Ray through the hospital, which was now noisy and bustling. Ray complied automatically, moving slowly on legs that felt leaden. "Are you okay to drive home?" asked Damien. "I'd offer to drive you, but there's the little matter of your patrol car. It's a little too conspicuous to leave it in the parking lot all day."

"Yeah. Some nitwit with poor impulse control just wouldn't be able to resist fucking with it," Ray replied. Christ, his voice had that hoarse sound of exhaustion. "You can ride home in the patrol car with me and talk to me so I stay awake. If my driving gets erratic, you can pinch me." Ray chuckled as Damien guided him into a small office. He could feel himself getting punchy.

Damien looked like he was searching his mind for a good comeback, as they both gathered up their personal gear. "No. You're making it just too easy," he muttered with a shake of his head. "I assume that if I ride home with you, you'll bring me back to get my car after we've gotten some sleep?"

"Of course!" Ray thought Damien's question was silly. Then again, he was so damn tired, he might not realize it made perfect sense.

"When we agree I'll ride home with you, *home* in this case is your house, right?"

Ray started to reply. He paused, remembering their conversation from early that morning. "For now, yeah. We can work out the long-term definition when we've both had some sleep."

Damien smiled. "You got a deal."

Ray gathered his gear, throwing his rucksack over one shoulder as Damien picked up his own bag. "Now let's get the hell out of here."

The drive to Ray's house took half an hour with the heavy traffic of the end of the morning commute. Damien immediately launched into a series of questions. Ray answered slowly, concentrating on his driving. He appreciated Damien's effort to keep him awake, and the conversation made the drive go by faster.

Ray pulled into his garage, parking the patrol car beside his personal vehicle. They retrieved their rucksacks from the trunk and headed for the inside door. As Ray activated the automatic garage door, he unlocked the inner door to the house. Punching in his alarm code stopped the high-pitched tone. When Damien closed the door and turned the deadbolt, silence descended over them.

It was eerie. Ray was used to Harley being somewhere nearby, even the previous times Damien had been here. He had a routine he usually followed and wasn't sure what to do with himself now. He set his gear down on the kitchen floor just inside the door. It was strange, not having to let Harley out into the backyard or fill his water bowl. He had Damien to focus on, he reminded himself.

"Do you need anything to drink? Are you hungry?" Ray asked, retrieving himself a bottle of water from the fridge. He held it up in invitation for Damien, finding him slumped in a chair at the small kitchen table.

"Water would be great," Damien replied. "But I'm not hungry."

Ray extended a hand to Damien, using it to haul him to his feet. Damien took the bottle of water Ray offered him, drinking from it greedily.

"Let's get you into bed," Ray said, retrieving his rucksack and throwing it over his shoulder. He miscalculated the turn into his own bedroom, clipping the doorjamb with his shoulder.

"I'll get you settled first, so you don't fall and break something by tripping over me." Damien's voice was filled with humor. Ray didn't have the energy to object to being the butt of the joke. "What do you need to do? Change your clothes? Brush your teeth?" he asked, turning down Ray's bed.

Ray watched Damien, feeling the same sense of intimacy he always did when they spent their nights together. "I need a shower," he replied. Ray gathered the clean clothes he'd need after he showered. He didn't typically wear that much to sleep, and with Damien in the house, he would probably not wear anything.

Looking up, Ray found Damien watching him, looking curious. "Will you be okay on your own? Or should I stick around to make sure you don't fall asleep on your feet?"

"I think you should come with me," Ray answered. "Help me stay awake. I might need some help getting clean, too." He struggled to keep his expression smooth, while Damien laughed openly. Ray would never get tired of hearing Damien laugh, and of seeing him smile.

"No problem." Damien sat down on the edge of Ray's bed and started to remove his shoes.

Despite the dark circles of exhaustion beneath his eyes, Damien's expression was soft as he looked down from where he sat propped against the headboard.

Ray let the bedroom light spill into the bathroom. When he and Damien showered together after sex, this was how they kept the mood going. Getting clean wasn't typically all they did when they showered.

Turning on the taps to warm the water, Ray started getting things ready for Damien. He glanced at the vanity and felt the strange emptiness that usually accompanied Damien's departure at the end of the weekend. He'd taken to keeping extra clean towels out, ready for anytime Damien came to visit. It was probably time for each of them to have space permanently set aside in each other's houses. Ray liked the idea of Damien's toothbrush always being beside his.

Toeing off his shoes, Ray stripped off his T-shirt. He was naked when Damien stepped in, filling the small room with his presence. As Damien placed his Dopp kit on the vanity, Ray reached for him, tugging impatiently at his scrubs.

Damien's laugh was muffled by his shirt as Ray pulled it over his head. "Impatient," he mumbled through laughter and fabric.

"I'm eager to celebrate with you," Ray said, smiling in response. He snaked his arm around Damien's waist, pulling him in close. His warmth and scent filled Ray's senses, his cock beginning to fill in response. "I'm relieved that Harley looks like he's going to be okay. I wanna have some fun with you before I fall asleep standing up."

Damien came eagerly, warm and pliant as he pressed his body against Ray's. "I guarantee I can keep you awake," he whispered against Ray's lips, and then covered his mouth in a full kiss.

Ray groaned, pulling Damien flush against his length. He opened up at the first sweep of Damien's tongue. Skimming his palms over the heated skin of Damien's back and shoulders, Ray felt the shift of his firm muscles. Pressing his hips against Damien's, Ray dragged his semirigid cock along warm, silky skin. Damien teased Ray, licking playfully at his tongue, nipping at his lower lip.

Fumbling blindly, Ray managed to open the shower door. Gripping Damien's firm ass cheeks, Ray tried to guide him beneath the spray. It'd be a hell of a lot easier to do if he broke their kiss, but Ray was reluctant to sacrifice that contact. Damien pressed his erection against Ray's hip, sliding them against one another sensuously. Ray's own hard-on throbbed with the beat of his heart, like it was straining to get inside of Damien's body.

Impatience roaring over him, Ray tore his mouth from Damien's. He stepped under the warm spray of water, using his grip on Damien's ass to compel him to follow. Ray pressed open-mouthed kisses to Damien's throat as water cascaded over them. Tilting his head back, leaving himself open, Damien rubbed the length his body against Ray's, clinging to his shoulders with strong fingers.

As Ray closed them inside the stall, steam rose up and swirled around them. Damien's harsh breathing carried over the rushing flow of water. His moans of pleasure echoed off the tiled walls, reverberating through Ray's chest. As rushing water spilled over them, heat seeped into Ray's muscles. His body relaxed as the tension of the long night finally eased. Again, he realized just how indebted he was to Damien.

Ray stood Damien beneath the full rush of water, watching it spill down his tall frame. Running his fingers through Damien's hair, he ensured each strand was saturated. Rivulets of water poured down Damien's dark skin, tempting Ray to trace the same paths with his tongue. He struggled to focus on getting them both clean, but his desire made it as difficult as always.

Damien's dark hair was thick, but Ray needed only a small amount of shampoo to build a sensuous lather. The look of bliss on Damien's face was a treat. Ray worked to ease Damien's tension, using his fingertips to caress and massage. The moan Damien released was decadent, as the taut muscles of his neck surrendered to Ray's touch.

It was such a pleasure to watch Damien bask in the well-earned pampering, Ray couldn't contain his own smile. With the lather rinsed from his hair, Damien opened his eyes. His lids were heavy, his pupils blown wide with desire. Ray's cock throbbed with a fresh rush of blood, aching to push up inside Damien's tight heat.

Gently guiding docile, yielding Damien from beneath the spray, Ray lathered a cloth with shower gel. Even as he encouraged Damien's muscles to loosen, Ray smoothed the cloth over his sensitized skin. Damien's skin pebbled with gooseflesh as Ray softly swiped the cloth over places he knew drove Damien mad. He'd done a great deal of recon during their time together, and Ray put it to good use now. The underside of Damien's bicep, his ribcage, and the centerline of his abdomen were sensitive to the lightest touch. Gasping and writhing, Damien submitted to the caresses of Ray's cloth-covered hand. He particularly enjoyed the way Damien's nipples hardened with the barest of touches. Wrapping his arms around Damien's trim waist, Ray moved the cloth over his back and shoulders. Damien lowered his head, resting his forehead on Ray's shoulder. With his arms around Ray's shoulders, Damien rocked against him, their slick skin letting them slide easily against each other.

There was no resistance as Ray guided Damien back beneath the warm spray. His system was jolted by the brush of his cock against Damien's, fueling his impatience. Ray let the flowing water rinse the lather from Damien's skin, even as he poured more gel into his palm. He reached between Damien's thighs, grasping his hard-on with one hand, cradling his heavy sac with the other.

"Oh fuck!" Damien exclaimed breathlessly. His grip on Ray's biceps was bruising as his entire body vibrated. "Jesus Christ, I love when you touch me." Damien's whisper was almost lost in the torrent of water.

Ray stroked Damien's cock lightly, feeling the pulse of his heart in his hardened shaft. He lathered Damien's ball sac, reaching even farther past with a soap-covered hand. As he washed Damien thoroughly, Ray teased him a little, hinting at the pleasure yet to come.

Tightening his hand on Damien's erection, Ray increased his rhythm. He wanted to take the edge off, get Damien nice and relaxed before spreading him open across the bed. With his other hand, Ray circled Damien's hole, teasing his clenched opening with his fingertips, but not pushing in yet.

Damien suddenly gripped Ray's wrists, surprising him by stilling his movements. "No, no, no, no," he said in a hoarse voice, the grasp of his fingers firm. "I know what you're trying to do. You're always so damn bossy." Damien gave a low chuckle. "You can give it up and relax, for one night, at least."

Ray froze, resting his temple against Damien's. He breathed heavily through parted lips, suddenly afraid he'd fucked things up in a way he hadn't seen coming. Releasing his wrists, Damien deftly steered Ray beneath the shower. He scrubbed at what little hair Ray sported, getting him clean. Studying Damien, Ray thought he looked a little smug as well as turned on. Maybe he wasn't really angry and Ray hadn't actually fucked up.

"Don't look so damn serious," Damien said with a husky voice. One corner of his mouth lifted in a teasing smile. "There's no great mystery to solve. Just lay back and enjoy all the dirty things I'm gonna do to you."

Ray could do that; no problem. He closed his eyes and concentrated on Damien's hands, gliding over his skin. Even the coarseness of the cloth felt good along sensitive patches of skin. The steam swirling around them carried the clean, spiced scent of the shower gel. He knew it was his imagination, but Ray thought he could feel the last tendrils of fear sluice off his body and spin down the drain. His tension rinsed away, along with any lingering grime and sweat. Damien was sensitive and discreet, but Ray knew when he was cleaning off residual smudges of Harley's blood from Ray's skin. He felt cleaner—lighter—as Damien held him steady beneath the deluge.

Despite his exhaustion, and the fucked up night they'd both had, Ray's dick didn't seem any worse for wear. Damien grasped him with soap-slick hands, dragging Ray to the edge with just a few determined strokes.

Damien let his mouth hover just above Ray's, his breath teasing Ray's lips. "I think you're all nice and clean now," he murmured, dragging his tongue over Ray's lower lip. "It's time I got you tucked up into bed."

"Getting tucked in isn't what I had in mind," Ray replied, unable to mask his smirk. He gripped Damien's hips, pulled him close, and rubbed the lengths of their stiff shafts together.

"Well, isn't that convenient then?" Damien nipped at Ray's throat as he reached to shut off the water.

Hardly noticing the slightly chilled air, Ray let himself be dried off. Damien was brisk and efficient, toweling all the moisture from Ray's skin. He was placid and acquiescent, letting Damien lead him from the bathroom, and over to the bed. Shutting off the bedroom light, Damien left the hallway light burning, casting the bedroom in a soft glow. Ray thought it was perfect; not too bright, but enough illumination for him to see Damien clearly.

Yanking back the covers, Damien cleared the bed for their use. He was focused and determined, making it easy for Ray to surrender. He laid back onto the pillows, opening his arms and legs for Damien to settle on top of him.

Ray wrapped his legs around Damien's waist, rocking his hips to slide their shafts along each other. He curled his arms around Damien's torso, bringing their chests together. Ray arched his neck upward, hungrily chasing Damien's mouth for a kiss.

It was fucking frustrating, the way Damien kept his lips just out of Ray's reach. With a growl, low in his throat, Ray nipped sharply at the warm skin beneath Damien's earlobe. Rubbing himself against Damien's body, he felt a teasing laugh from deep in Damien's chest. Ray grasped Damien's ass with both hands, pulling him closer and holding him steady. Rocking his hips, rubbing his cock against Damien's body, Ray wordlessly urged Damien to keep teasing, touching, kissing—whatever felt good.

Carding his fingers through Damien's silky hair, Ray gripped handfuls of dark strands. He steadied Damien's head, determined to take a deep kiss. Ray needed to see Damien's eyes looking into his own, as he felt him push into his ass. His memories of last night; the second-guessing, and borrowing trouble, were scattered to the wind. Damien already flooded Ray's senses, now he dominated his conscious thoughts. Of course, bodies and emotions would follow.

Damien hovered over Ray, braced on his arms. He smiled playfully down at Ray, wetting his lower lip with the tip of his tongue. Damien thrust his hips hard against Ray's ass, slipping his cock along Ray's crease. The feel of Damien nudging Ray's hole with his cockhead dragged a low moan from deep inside him. Ray was done waiting for Damien get them both prepped.

Letting go of Damien's ass, Ray twisted beneath him, reaching for the drawer of the bedside table. "Supplies," he blurted.

Ray was startled when Damien grabbed his wrist in a firm grip. "Slow down," Damien said in a low, seductive voice. Ray's cock pulsed once with interest as he tested Damien's intent and resolve. "Always in such a damn hurry." Damien murmured. He moved Ray's arm up, pressing his wrist into the pillow beneath his head. "Why don't you lay back? Relax. Just live in the moment, before you analyze it into boredom. Just *feel* what we do, before you *think* all the intimacy and pleasure out of us."

Looking closely, Ray saw Damien's expression was relaxed and genuine. He took a breath, lowered his legs from Damien's waist, and let himself melt into the bed beneath them. They stretched out against each other, legs twining. The usual urgency was missing; the familiar desperation to be physically connected.

Damien's words were enough of a surprise, but Ray was more startled to feel how much tension bled from his own body. He hadn't been aware he always rushed them, always chased their mutual pleasure. He'd believed they had to touch, to be physically connected, for them to share intimacy.

Smiling softly, Damien lowered himself onto his forearms. His eyes were open wide, probably able to see Ray clearly. "Yeah. Just like that," Damien whispered. "Let me make you feel good. No expectations. No obligations."

Ray gasped, his chest tightened with a sharp ache. Damien scared him, with his forthright honesty, and no demands. Lifting a trembling hand to Damien's face, Ray cupped his cheek, stroking his thumb over flushed skin. "Okay," Ray whispered his surrender. Emotions chased across Damien's expression, leaving no doubt as to how he felt about Ray. "If that's what you want." He'd been chasing after something they already had.

Lowering his head, Damien nuzzled Ray's earlobe. He huffed a quiet laugh, his breath warm as it ghosted over the shell of Ray's ear. All of Damien was warm, where he was pressed against Ray. "I want to do what you like to do; what you enjoy," he whispered. Damien placed soft, wet kisses along the length of Ray's neck, nipping gently at the join of his shoulder.

Ray moaned, his body quaking in pleasure. Christ, Damien had a special talent for taking away all of Ray's control over his own body. Turning his face slightly, he wordlessly begged Damien never to stop. Damien obliged him, tracing that sensitive tendon of his neck with stinging bites. Ray clutched reflexively at Damien, desperate to anchor himself here, to the moment. He dug his fingers into Damien's waist and held on, trusting him to secure Ray to him.

Damien rocked against him, grinding their hips together rhythmically. Ray eagerly pushed his hips upward, meeting Damien's body, matching his rhythm. Their erections were cradled between them, the pressure and friction narrowing Ray's focus. They were all alone in the universe—together.

Damien's cock lay against Ray's lower belly, thick and heavy. It glided along their sweat-slick skin as they rocked and thrust against each other. The skin of Damien's stomach was smooth and hot against Ray's erection and coated in a light sheen of sweat. Ray flexed his hips upward into Damien's firm thrusts. The thick vein on the underside of his hard-on slid against Damien's stomach, sending pleasure rolling through Ray's body in warm waves. Caressing Damien's calves with his own, Ray urged him to move faster. He grasped Damien's hips, using his grip to bring their bodies together with more force.

"Slow it down again," Damien said quietly, his voice rough with desire. "We're gonna get there. Let's just take our time." His eyes were heavy lidded, but Ray still saw glimmers of passion and affection. Damien teased him with soft, biting kisses to his lower lip, easing the sting with a gentle flick of his tongue.

Ray hadn't known until tonight that teasing was so fucking arousing. He enjoyed Damien's mouth on him and loved it more when Damien exploited that intel. Pulling back out of reach, Damien broke kiss after kiss. Ray was embarrassed by the impatient and frustrated sounds he made as he chased Damien's mouth, desperate to recapture his lips. Damien never lost his teasing grin as he evaded Ray playfully, staying just out of reach.

Letting his head fall back onto his pillow, Ray gave a quiet growl. This little game was fun—his throbbing dick was proof of that—but it was time Damien got a taste of his own medicine. "I really pissed you the hell off, huh?" he said jokingly, watching for the moment Damien became distracted. "You really fucking enjoy punishing me." Ray started to reverse their positions, but Damien was on to him.

"I'm not punishing you," Damien declared firmly, "and you fucking know it." His smile held a small hint of smugness as he resisted Ray's attempt to turn the tables. "In fact, I've got you all turned on." For emphasis, Damien pushed his body forcefully against Ray's, slowly sliding up his entire length.

A rush of blood, fresh and warm, flooded Ray's cock as Damien rubbed against him. He couldn't stop his hips from pushing up into Damien. He slid his erection against Damien's hip, and along his taut stomach. A wonderful tension coiled low in Ray's belly and Damien hadn't even touched a hand to his dick.

"So let me return the favor," Ray said breathlessly. "I can help you get your dick nice and hard." He smiled up at Damien, silently issuing a playful challenge. Damien didn't need any help, since he was rubbing his full erection against Ray's. "Then we can really start having some fun."

Ray started to open his legs, already guiding Damien to settle between them. "We already were having fun," Damien replied. He reached for Ray's arms, gently but insistently moving them upward toward the pillows. "You just need to remember how to be patient."

Before Ray could think of a witty reply, before he could show any resistance, Damien pressed his face to Ray's throat. As his moan became a simple sigh of pleasure, Ray relaxed back down into the bed. His pulse point danced with his rapidly beating heart until Damien covered the sensitive patch of skin with parted lips. Ray tried to reach for Damien, to pull his heated body in close again, but Damien stopped him with a caressing grip on his forearms. Ray's heart rate leapt up several gears, making his blood rush in his ears. With his lips pressed to the hammering pulse in Ray's throat, Damien drew on it with gentle pressure, teasing it with a light flick of his tongue.

Closing his eyes, Ray arched his neck so Damien could do anything he wanted. The feel of Damien's fingers lightly tracing a path up toward his wrist sent a shiver of pleasure humming through his body. When Damien's palm cradled the back of his hand, Ray twined their fingers distractedly. Damien's lips against his palm were startling. It was nice, the way warmth coursed up the length of his arm. Opening his eyes, Ray found he was being watched. Damien's expression held no traces of his previous humor as he met Ray's eyes without blinking.

With one hand, he held Ray's palm against his own cheek. With his other hand, Damien gently traced his fingertips over the tattoo on Ray's forearm—the brightly colored memory of Saija. Damien's expression was soft, filled with deep affection. He looked as happy as Ray felt. The energy that surrounded them, that surged through both of them, felt very different now. Their physical desire was still mutual, and powerful, but it meant something different to them now.

Shifting slightly on the bed, Ray gently adjusted Damien's position. He pulled Damien's body against his own, using his free arm in a steady embrace. Damien kept the fingers of their joined hands twined. He didn't hide his feelings, letting Ray see everything he was feeling, including his vulnerability. The small knot returned to Ray's stomach, so did the tightness in his chest. Again, Damien caressed Ray's forearm, focusing on the tattoo for Saija. It wasn't the ink alone he revered, Ray finally realized. Damien admired and respected Ray's injury, along with his dedication to his dogs.

Suddenly, his throat tightened, a painful lump forming. Ray knew his expression mirrored Damien's identically.

He couldn't hide all of these intense, tumultuous feelings he had for Damien; they were too obvious. What surprised him was that he didn't care; he didn't want to keep everything bottled up, he wanted it out there so everyone would know. Ray wanted to share his happiness with everyone in his life.

For now, though, he wanted to show Damien just what he meant to Ray. After last night, they both needed reassurance that each of them had come through it all okay. With their talk this morning, it was time to seal their bond and to move forward together.

Ray was just about to speak when Damien seemed to read his mind. He rose up, once again holding himself over Ray's body. He kissed Ray, long and deep. Ray licked back into Damien's mouth, his hunger and enthusiasm ruling them both, turning the kiss wet and messy.

Damien finally broke the kiss, but Ray wasn't ready for it to end. He lifted himself toward Damien, trying to recapture his mouth. Ray had to settle for mouthing a path along Damien's throat, while he fumbled through the drawer of the bedside table. A shiver ran through his frame and Damien swore as he clumsily dropped some items onto the bed.

Snatching them up, Ray chuckled at the entire strip of condoms Damien had retrieved. "You're really optimistic," he said, holding the foil packets up between them. "Just which one of us has such unrealistic expectations to live up to?"

Damien rolled his eyes. He snatched the strip from Ray, using his teeth to tear off a single condom. He tossed the rest back into the drawer, sliding it shut forcefully. "It's hard to do this shit with only one hand," he said around the foil in his teeth.

Ray laughed, taking the condom from Damien. "I'm happy to help." He set the condom aside and flicked open the lid of the lubricant bottle. He coated a finger and reached between their bodies.

Circling his finger around the rim of his asshole, Ray began to spread the lube. Damien rose up onto his knees, giving Ray an incredulous look. "You're not going to do all the fun stuff by yourself, are you?"

Ray pictured Damien pushing two lubed fingers into him and his hole spasmed with excitement. "Well, you were having a little trouble, so I thought I'd help."

Damien quickly coated one of his own fingers with lube. He reached behind Ray's balls and nudged his hand away. Ray obliged him, drawing his knees upward in anticipation. Unerringly, Damien found Ray's sensitive opening with his own slick finger. Their eyes met and locked, each gazing steadily at the other's face.

The strong, steady push of Damien's finger into Ray's hole sent a fission up the length of his spine. Arching his back, Ray delighted in the extreme pleasure he always felt with the first penetration. He breathed deeply, keeping his eyes on Damien's face. Twisting his wrist, Damien spread the lube inside of Ray, teasing all the sensitive nerve endings.

Sliding his finger free, Damien quickly covered two fingers with slick. He teased Ray's opening with his fingertips, circling it several times. Damien pushed firmly, and Ray's body opened for him easily. With a small smile of pleasure, Ray sucked his breath in through his teeth. Damien smiled down at him affectionately, pushing his fingers deep into Ray's ass.

Damien added more slick to his fingers. Ray was already so relaxed, his hole didn't resist Damien's touch. He took Damien's two fingers into his ass eagerly, lifting his hips, silently begging for more. Ray was sure his hole was well lubed, and he was ready for more. He wanted all of Damien inside him.

"You're so relaxed already," said Damien in a hoarse whisper. "I just need to be sure you're nice and slick, so we both have a smooth ride." He doused three fingers with lube. Obviously done teasing, Damien pushed his fingers past Ray's opening, sliding deep into his ass.

With a moan of pleasure, Ray thrust his hips several times. He took Damien's fingers deeper, enjoying how they pressed and rubbed on all the sensitive spots inside. "With you, I don't need a lot of encouragement," Ray said with a grin. He found the condom among the bedding, tearing it open with his teeth.

He watched Damien retrieve the lube and flick open the lid. Ray gripped the tip of the latex, positioning it over the swollen head of Damien's erection. He barely had it rolled down to the base before Damien was adding a final coat of lubricant.

Ray drew his knees upward as Damien reached between their bodies. Aligning his cockhead with Ray's asshole, Damien pushed himself inward relentlessly. He was hard and unyielding, pressed to Ray's sensitive hole. He breathed deep and steady as Damien thrust his hips, nudging his hard-on deeper into Ray's ass. As his body opened, easily taking Damien in, Ray lifted his arms and clasped the back of Damien's head with both hands.

He held Damien steady, their gazes locked. Ray moaned loudly, unashamed at the wanton sound. As Damien filled his ass, he stared deep into Ray's eyes. Ray loved the feel of Damien's cock stretching his hole. The inner muscles of his ass firmly gripped Damien's erection, impatiently drawing him in deeper.

There was no hiding for either of them, no guarding their feelings, no masking their emotions. Ray saw Damien's vulnerability clearly, saw his desperate need to give Ray pleasure. So many of the emotions that Ray saw in Damien's eyes echoed in his own chest. Cradling Damien's face in his palms, he watched his expression flow between bliss and gratification. Ray canted his hips, taking Damien the rest of the way in. He shouted softly as Damien's cock filled his ass completely.

For several long moments neither of them moved, Ray's body growing accustomed to Damien's erection inside him. The skin of Damien's hips and thighs was slick with sweat and heated where he pressed himself tight against Ray's ass cheeks. Damien released a shaky breath, his eyes boring deep into Ray's. With Damien's face still firmly clasped, his deepest thoughts and feelings were there for Ray to see.

His open expression spoke louder than words, telling Ray unequivocally that Damien's feelings for him were deep and strong. With his brow slightly furrowed, Damien pulled his hips back slowly. Ray inhaled sharply, suddenly feeling empty. The flare of Damien's cockhead caught the rim of Ray's asshole, stretching it a little more and coaxing out a small gasp of pleasure. He lifted his hips, meeting Damien's firm thrust. Ray gave a broken moan as Damien pushed into him again, filling his ass, their bodies meeting audibly.

The way Damien looked at him—saw *into* him—was such a fucking turn-on. Ray's cock throbbed, his balls tightened and pulsed in time with his heartbeat. He could probably come without either of them touching his dick, as long as Damien was looking at him just like *that*. Ray understood—he *knew*—what it was Damien felt, and how desperate he was to please Ray, to make him happy.

Christ, he was so fucking lucky to be on the receiving end of Damien's attentions. Ray was laid bare before Damien, wide open and completely vulnerable. For two violent beats of his heart, Ray felt a powerful urge to close his eyes, and turn away. Damien kept his gaze steady though, working his cock in and out of Ray's ass. There was no way in hell he could look away now. Ray worked his hips against Damien's, sliding him out quickly, taking him in, deep and quick. He left himself wide open, letting Damien see the strength of Ray's feelings, and their mutual vulnerability.

Damien gave him a watery smile. Lowering himself onto Ray's body, Damien chuffed a short laugh that might have been a joyful sob. Ray circled his arms around Damien's shoulders, holding their bodies together. Gripping Damien's hips between his open thighs, Ray pushed and pulled against his body. He breathed harshly against Damien's damp skin, gasping and moaning when Damien's cock pressed and rubbed against more sensitive places.

Ray's cock ached, rubbing against Damien's belly as they moved and strained against each other. He wanted to reach between their bodies, grip his own hard-on, and finish himself. Those thoughts fled when Damien shifted, thrusting himself even deeper into Ray's ass. Sparks cascaded behind his eyelids each time Damien glanced over Ray's gland. He wanted to murmur in Damien's ear, tell him how fucking good this felt, but the words were trapped in his tightened throat.

Damien thrust hard, his cock pushing right against Ray's sweet spot. Ray shouted his pleasure, his own erection leaving wet smears on both their stomachs. He clutched desperately at Damien's shoulders, burying his fingers in firm muscle. Again and again, Damien teased his cock over Ray's gland, dragging them both relentlessly toward the climatic edge.

It was a surprise, and a relief, when Damien slowed his thrusts. Ray shivered as Damien pushed back into him slowly. He rubbed his legs against Damien's in agitation, pulled impatiently at his hips. Ray was damn near ready to beg Damien to resume his punishing rhythm.

"Easy, easy," Damien whispered. His breath was hot against the shell of Ray's ear. "Do you feel good?" He skimmed his palms soothingly along Ray's sides. His beard was pleasantly rough against Ray's skin as he rubbed their cheeks together. "I wanna make you feel good. You enjoy this?"

Ray nodded in reply, nosing along Damien's jawline. He didn't want to talk, he wanted Damien to move like he had been; faster and harder. He moved restlessly, arching up into Damien.

"God, I love how you feel against me." Damien moved his hips slowly, sliding his hands all over Ray's body. "Just touching you, I can tell how strong you are. I get hard when I think about running my fingers through your chest hair." The humor in his voice, the way he buried his face against Ray's neck, made him think Damien was embarrassed by his heartfelt confessions.

Gently, Ray smoothed his palms up and down Damien's back. He slowed his own pace to match Damien's, instead of demanding more. "I get hard when I think about your smile, or the color of your eyes," he whispered, smiling against Damien's shoulder. "It feels good to be with you." Ray didn't want Damien to doubt anything that was between the two of them.

Damien stroked into him deeper, moving faster and harder. He rose up over Ray slightly, nuzzling at his temple. His rapid breathing danced warmly over Ray's cheek. He sensed a tension in Damien that went beyond the enjoyment of sex.

"Does this feel good to you?" Damien asked breathlessly. "Do you enjoy this? Do I make you feel good? Are you...happy?"

Damien's final word was nearly lost in Ray's own cry of pleasure. With a deep thrust, Damien angled his hips to push his cock hard against Ray's gland. His stomach tightened and his heart swelled when the question registered in Ray's mind, when he realized what Damien needed to know. Ray wrapped one arm around Damien's back. He used his physical strength to pull Damien close, connecting their bodies at as many points as he could. Carding his fingers through Damien's sweaty hair, Ray gripped a fistful of the damp strands.

"I love being with you," Ray whispered against Damien's cheek. His voice broke each time Damien buried his cock deep inside Ray. "Feels so fucking good. *You* make me feel so fucking good."

Damien's movements became erratic as he slammed his cock in and out of Ray's hole. He clung frantically to Ray, his breathing rapid and harsh. Smiling to himself, Ray closed his eyes and rode the waves of pleasure coursing through his body.

"Oh fuck," Damien growled. "Fuck yeah." Each time he buried his dick deep, Damien hammered Ray's sweet spot. "I love the sweet feel of your ass around my cock. So fucking nice."

This was just what Ray had been wanting. He held tight, losing himself in the dual sensation of Damien sliding deep into his ass and sliding against his dick. Ray's hard-on was leaking continuously now, leaving wet smears along his skin. Damien fucked into him several more times, and Ray's aching cock pulsed and swelled.

"I'm gonna come," Damien said, his voice rising in pitch. "I'm so fucking close. Want you to come with me. Wanna come together."

Ray was close too; it wouldn't take much. "Don't stop," he gasped, "Don't stop." He kept his eyes shut tight. Damien's scent, the heat of his body made something pleasant coil low in Ray's belly, tightening his sac and drawing his balls up close. "Like this. Just like this." He clutched at Damien, pulling him close and holding their bodies together tightly. Ray slid his bare skin against Damien's, arching upward to get contact everywhere he could reach. "Wanna touch..." He struggled to remember the words. "Just...touch me...please." Damien would know what he meant.

Slowly shifting his body against Ray's, Damien settled over him. Gooseflesh rose on his skin at Damien's sensual touches. He sighed in pleasure, Damien's heated chest scorching against his own. "Wrap yourself around me," Damien said in a hoarse whisper. Gently caressing Ray's thigh, Damien guided it around his own waist. "Hold tight to me...gonna take care of you..."

Ray eagerly wrapped both legs around Damien, holding onto him with equal parts affection and desperation. Slipping his arms beneath Ray, Damien cradled him like he was something precious. With his face pressed to Ray's temple, Damien flexed his hips, sliding his cock almost completely free. Reflexively tightening his hold on Damien frame, Ray made a sound of protest.

Damien murmured words of comfort and encouragement, thrusting his hips downward. Ray shouted with pleasure as Damien's cock filled his ass, pressing relentlessly on his sensitive gland. His own erection leaked more fluid onto his skin, his ball sac growing tight again. Damien withdrew himself smoothly, plunging back in before Ray caught his breath.

Overwhelmed by so many sensations, Ray's body quaked as he lay clinging to Damien. His toes were curled, each push of Damien's cock to Ray's sweet spot pulled involuntary cries from his throat. He could just hear the steady torrent of words Damien spoke against Ray's skin. The words of affection and encouragement affected Ray as powerfully as Damien's movements inside his body. His cock throbbed, his balls drew up close to his body. Racing with Damien, Ray reached the edge of the cliff. Damien thrust into Ray's ass, encouraging Ray to topple off the peak with him.

Ray arched his back, a bright shower of sparks cascading behind his eyelids. His cry of pleasure caught in his throat as Ray quickly followed Damien over the cliff. His body vibrated around Damien's cock buried deep inside him. His own cock pulsed violently, hot fluid flowing between them, coating the skin of their stomachs. Ray finally caught his breath, his shouts of pleasure melding with Damien's joyful cries. Damien's cock, buried deep inside Ray, twitched and pulsed as he spilled into Ray's ass. Their bodies were pressed tightly together, capturing Ray's seed between them.

Damien held him in a tight embrace, his strong arms wrapped firmly around Ray. They rode the waves of their shared orgasms, holding tight to each other. Ray loved the feel of Damien in and around him, shaking violently with the force of his climax. He was sure some of Damien's shouts became sobs of pleasure, and Ray couldn't help a small sense of triumph. He'd never felt this intimate, this connected to another person. Ray couldn't get the words out, which would express what he felt for Damien, and how deep those feelings went. He stayed wrapped around Damien's body, hoping he could feel all the things Ray couldn't say.

It seemed to take forever before the power of his orgasm began to release him. Ray finally relaxed down onto the bed. Opening his eyes, he blinked several times despite his heavy eyelids. A violent aftershock caught Ray by surprise, his inner muscles clamping down on Damien's softening cock. He gasped against Ray's temple, an answering quake vibrating through Damien's body. With their bodies still intimately joined, they lay together as they slowly came down from the highs of their powerful climaxes.

Ray was getting drowsy as his body finally relaxed completely. He rubbed soothingly at Damien's back as occasional aftershocks still rolled through him. He hardly felt Damien's weight when he finally collapsed onto Ray's body. Closing his eyes, Ray kept his arms wrapped around Damien, slipping into a light doze.

Damien gently jostled Ray awake as he carefully pulled out of his arms. His limbs felt like lead as Damien untangled them from each other. "You ready?" Damien whispered, reaching between their bodies to where they were joined.

"Yeah," Ray answered, taking a deep breath. He grunted at the discomfort of Damien sliding his softened cock free of Ray's ass. He felt strangely empty and suddenly bereft without Damien inside him. He'd never been left feeling this way before. When Damien left him to deal with the condom, Ray closed his eyes, trying to ignore his strange feelings.

When he heard the shower running, Ray assumed Damien was showering. With his own come drying on his skin, and lubricant still in some sensitive places, Ray thought a shower was a good idea. He just couldn't get his eyes to open, or his body to move.

Damien was suddenly back, carrying a wet hand towel. It was warm on his skin when Damien used it to clean the drying come from Ray's stomach. His melancholy eased at Damien's first touch, which didn't really surprise Ray.

"Here," Damien said quietly as he gently repositioned Ray's leg, "Stay right like this for me. Just for a minute." He was thorough but loving, carefully cleaning Ray of sweat, and the last traces of lube. He finally straightened Ray's leg, giving him a final, affectionate pat. "All done. You can relax now," Damien said, disappearing into the bathroom.

Ray awakened to the feel of the bed dipping beneath him. He opened his eyes to total darkness, but he could make out Damien's form, moving beside him. Ray hooked his arm around Damien's narrow waist, tugging him down. There wasn't much difference in size between them, but they still managed to sleep comfortably with Damien draped across him, his head cradled on Ray's chest. Turning to press a kiss to the top of Damien's head, Ray inhaled the pleasant scents of shampoo, sweat, and something lightly spicy that was unique to Damien. He couldn't think of any reason to move.

Taking a deep breath, Ray rolled his shoulders and shook out his hands. If he didn't relax, he was going to end up sending his tension down leash. Harley sat right beside him, eyes on his face, eagerly waiting for his first command.

"How are you doing?" Damien asked softly. He stood right at Ray's shoulder, a steady source of unquestioning support. "You know Harley's up for this. Everything will be fine." With confidence visible in everything about him, Ray had complete faith in Damien.

"If you say he's ready, he's ready," replied Ray. Damien had designed a plan for Harley's rehab and conditioning, and Ray trusted him completely. "I'm just scared *I'll* be the reason we fuck up." He was sure he was rusty and was going to let everyone down.

Ray's hand was enveloped in warmth. He curled his fingers around Damien's, warmth spreading up his arm, and unfurling in his chest. Turning toward Damien, Ray smiled his thanks.

"Hurry up and get this over with, so you can take me to dinner on our way home." Damien glanced around them, feigning disinterest.

Like he knew Damien had planned, Ray's thoughts were on the friendly wager they'd laid between the two of them. "You just might be buying *me* dinner on our way home." Either way, Ray was going to come out a winner.

Damien chuckled in response, giving Ray's fingers a squeeze.

Movement in front of them captured Ray's attention. Releasing Damien's hand, he refocused on Harley, still sitting attentively beside him.

"Should I go sit down?" Damien asked. "Or do you want me to wait here for you?"

No matter how things went with Harley, Ray knew he'd want to talk to Damien right away. "Wait here," he replied definitively.

"I'll be right here when you're done." Damien took several steps back, giving Ray and Harley enough space to get themselves focused.

At the signal, Ray started forward. Harley was right on his heel, just like he should be. His fur had grown in to cover his scar, and a quick glance told Ray that Harley was moving comfortably. He'd been right to have faith in Damien's opinion.

Ray and Harley entered the arena, as the disembodied voice of the announcer introduced them to the crowd. Several camera shutters clicked as the media documented Harley's re-certification, and his return to patrol duty.

"Ladies and gentlemen, this next team is not only our two-time winner of the Top Dog title, but this past year, they distinguished themselves through their heroism. We're especially lucky to have Harley back with us after he was critically wounded in the line of duty. So, let's all let 'em know how glad we are to have them back. From the San Diego Sheriff's Department, it's Sergeant Ray Lerner, and his canine partner, Harley."

The End

Also by Kendall McKenna

The Recon Diaries
Brothers In Arms
Fire For Effect
The Final Line

Standalone
Waves Break My Fall
A Gentle Kind of Strength
Nights In Canaan
Fair Winds

Watch for more at https://www.facebook.com/authorkendallmckenna.